Zander

Erikson Brothers Book 6

Kathi S. Barton

This is a work of fiction. Names, characters, places, and incidents are products of the author's imagination or are used fictitiously and are not to be construed as real. Any resemblance to actual events, locations, organizations, or persons, living or dead, is entirely coincidental.

World Castle Publishing, LLC
Pensacola, Florida

Hardback ISBN: 9798246208564
Paperback ISBN: 9798891265127
eBook ISBN: 9798891265134
First Edition World Castle Publishing, LLC, March 9, 2026
http://www.worldcastlepublishing.com

Licensing Notes

Cover: Cover Designs by Karen
Editor: Karen Fuller

Chapter 1

It had been three days of no calls from someone who hadn't said anything. He was happy. Zander didn't want to have to change his phone number and go through all of that, but he would have if it had kept up. He was sick of getting them all hours of the day and night without anyone saying anything to him when he spoke. Most of the time, he would only say his last name, but they should have been answering when he said that. It was the least they could have done when they were calling him. Hopefully, he'd not have to worry about it again, and for that, he was thrilled.

He was going over some contracts for the family when Knox called him. They usually worked in the same building, both being lawyers for the family, but today he was having a shake-down of their new camper with his wife, and he'd asked for the day off. He was happy for Knox and Elaine. If anyone deserved some time off, it was the two of them. He leaned back in his chair to listen to his brother have a conversation with whom he could only assume was Elaine.

" I'm sure I have it right. It says right on the box where it's supposed to be plugged in. Didn't we plug it in here the last time we used the camper?" He didn't know what the other person was saying, but it must have been something along the lines of not knowing. " I'm sure that I had to plug it into this. If not, then I have no idea where it belongs. I knew I should have taken pictures of the things that we were using."

" Hello, Knox." The laughter on the other end had him smiling. " While I'm thrilled that you are having fun, I don't know where the plug goes either. What did you want?"

" I'm sorry about that. I get caught up in things when they're happening. I wanted to ask you if you'd gotten around to signing off on the contract from the bean company? They just called me to see if you'd gotten around to it. Is that one of the contracts that you decided to dump? I know there was one of them, but I don't remember which one it was." He said that they were dumping the coffee project. " That's the one with beans. I remember now. They wanted to buy land in another country and grow their own beans for coffee."

" That's it. They should have gotten their contract back yesterday, about us not wanting to take them on as an investment. I sent it by courier, and they signed for it yesterday. Sounds to me like they're trying to play us off one another." Knox said he wasn't surprised by that. They'd told him that he was their last hope. " I don't know how they expected anyone to finance their venture. It would be hard enough to buy the land, but getting the coffee beans to grow and then be picked would be expensive. I'm glad you did the search on them before it got too far."

" I am as well." There was a shuffling noise and then silence. He wondered if Knox had gone into his office and shut the door. As soon as he began speaking again, he knew that was what he'd done. " Did you hear about Allen Sharp? He was killed this morning when breakfast was being served. Something about him not liking the seats that were left over for him to sit at, and he got pissed. I guess it took them about an hour to figure out that he'd been stabbed three times before he was killed."

" I did hear about it, but I don't think that anyone has told Carrie yet. She'll be all right with the news if I know her very well. I know she's been sleeping better since he and the others had been put in prison awaiting trial." Knox said that he could tell her tonight, but was afraid that she'd hear about it through the grapevine, and that wouldn't be good.

Six months ago, Carrie Sharp had been working three jobs and taking care of her mother by herself. She had five brothers and three sisters who were about as bad as they came. They would beat her for her mother's social security check each month, telling Carrie she was going to have to do better for them to have the money. It was difficult enough for her to buy her mother's meds, much less put food on the table for the two of them at the same time. Allen had been by far the worst of them, and he'd beaten Carrie so bad once that she'd been in the hospital for a month and couldn't have children because of it.

They were all in prison now because they had forged the checks that had come to their mother and had beaten her up. Mrs. Sharp had end-stage Alzheimer's and was doing much better being in a nursing home where she could get round-the-clock care. Carrie worked for the family by writing programs and teaching people how to order their groceries online. She'd been terrified that some of her family would have gotten out of prison and killed her. That was what Allen had promised her the last day of court, which had sent him away.

" I can go over and tell her. I need to look some things up anyway." No doubt about how to use the plug that he had no idea where it went. " There are days when I can't believe that we bought ourselves a camper to see the country with and not have any idea what we're doing."

" You'll get it, I'm sure. You've only had it about a month now, right?" He said they'd gotten it exactly one month ago. " I think you're doing fine. Better than I would have. I'd have given up on the second day that

I had it. You guys have camped in it how many times now?"

" Four. We're getting better. This time, we decided to take it all down like we're moving and see if we could hook it up on our own. That didn't work out as well as we hoped." Then he laughed. " But we're having a blast, and that's what we bought it for. Who are you taking to the house tomorrow for Thanksgiving? You have a plus one invitation, correct?"

" I'm bringing Carrie. If she still wants to come after you talk to her." He said she'd be relieved about him being dead. " I'm sure she will be, but he's still her brother, and she might be a little upset."

" I don't know. I know that I'd be devastated if anything were to happen to any of you guys." He would as well and told him that. " I'm going to be leaving here soon. I do have to look up where the plug goes, and then we can decide if we need a couple more shakedowns. It's going to be fun if we ever figure this out. But that's fun as well. I'll tell you what she said, and if you want, I'll ask her about tomorrow." He said he'd call her later.

Carrie was a good friend of the family. Unlike what any of his brothers wanted, she wasn't going to be his wife. The other five had fallen in love with their wives within hours of meeting them. He and Carrie didn't have that kind of relationship, and he was sort of sad about it. She really was nice, and he did love her, but more like a sister than anything else.

Going on with his work, he was finished up by five o'clock. He might have been done sooner, but Carrie had called him, telling him that Allen had been killed. Like he figured, she didn't seem that upset with what had happened, and he was glad for her. She was still going with him to the family Thanksgiving at Locke's house tomorrow, and he was happy for that. She was fun to be around, and she had a good sense of humor about herself. He did love her like he'd said, but it was more like she was his sister than anything else.

Tomorrow, he was going to get his fill of food. Not that he didn't under normal circumstances, but since it was being catered, he didn't have to worry about having leftovers. He was thrilled that there were going to be other things other than turkey. He didn't care for it and was happy that Alex, Locke's wife, was going to have things like lasagna, too. He could eat his weight in that stuff and didn't care if they made fun of him while he did it.

On his way home, he thought of Carrie. He'd been doing that a lot since she'd come into their lives. He just couldn't get past the point where she felt like nothing to him that would make him think that he was madly in love with her, like his brothers did with their wives. He liked her a great deal, but nothing romantic at all. As soon as he got home, he decided that he was going to run for a while and changed into his jogging clothes. It was the perfect night out for a good long run, and he couldn't wait to get started.

He was nearly home again when he heard from August. Like Knox, he wanted to make sure that he knew that Allen had been killed. He told him that he knew now and was happy for it. He told him that even Carrie seemed to be happy about the turn of events, and he was happy for her as well. He asked him if he'd run into many people while out running.

" It was busy out. I'm not going to lie to you. It would have been better if there weren't stupid people out driving. Last-minute deals on food for tomorrow made the grocery store busier than normal, too. Their parking lot was full when I went by it." He asked if he was driving or walking over tomorrow. " Driving. I'll have to pick up Carrie, and I don't want her to get slush on her clothing."

" I'm going to walk. Jack said that we'll both need it after getting our fill, and I believe her. The same people who catered the Fourth of July are doing the food for Thanksgiving, and I'm excited for that. They make a great peanut butter pie that I love." He asked him if he ever thought about anything other than food. " Sure. I think about desserts and drinks to go with my food, too."

They both laughed, and August said he'd let him go and would see him tomorrow. Dinner was at five, but they were all supposed to show up at three. There would be finger food. He wanted real food, but could understand the need for little food too. There would be a lot of kids at the dinner, and they might not make it until dinner. He might not either, so he was looking forward to having something that he could munch on with the kids. He loved his nephews and niece very much.

Going to bed early, he wanted to go over the contracts for the new firm they were hiring in the morning, before going to his brothers'. It wasn't necessary to go over right away, but he hated to leave things last minute. January tenth was coming up fast to him, and he didn't want to leave things undone. Something might happen to him, and he didn't want anything to happen to the business if he was laid up.

At a quarter after three, he was picking up Carrie. She'd been running behind all morning and wasn't going to be ready by the three o'clock hour. He was fine with that. She'd called the family to let them know she was the one causing Zander to be late, and they were all right with it. Apparently, she'd been to see her mom at the nursing home, and she'd not had a good visit. As soon as she got into his car, she started apologizing to him.

" She didn't know me today, and I had such good news for her. I honestly didn't know how she'd take one of her children being dead, but I knew she was still having nightmares about Allen getting to her when she was with us." He asked her if she got to tell her. " I did end up telling her. She knew who he was if the fear on her face was any indication. They told me there that she still has nightmares where she wakes up screaming that he's got her. I know how she feels. I do the same thing myself."

" I can't imagine being so afraid of someone that you'd wish them dead. Especially when it's family." She said she'd never wish him to suffer, even though he did make people suffer when they didn't do what he wanted. " I'd die if something were to happen to one of my brothers. Or their wives. It would devastate me if that were to happen."

" You guys are incredibly close. I don't think I've ever seen a family as close as you guys are. It's wonderful to see, and sometimes I get really jealous about it." He told her that she had his family, too. " I know. I don't know what I would have done without them around all this time. I know for sure that I wouldn't have my mom in that nursing home. I wouldn't have been able to do it with them taking her checks each month. You also made it so that I could hide out, too, and if that hadn't happened, I'd be dead for sure. Those last weeks that Allen hadn't been arrested yet were the scariest times of my life. Just knowing that he was out there looking for me—and Syble, she would have turned me over to him had she been able to find me too—it gave me nightmares even during the day. I still think about how he said he was going to kill me while in the courtroom, and I nearly wet myself thinking about it. But he was put away, thanks to you and your family, and I can't thank you enough."

Dinner was epic. There was so much food that he was able to get his fill and have leftovers to take home as well. He'd be eating lasagna for a month daily if not for his family, and he was delighted about that. He even enjoyed the finger food with the kids. They thought of him as their greatest uncle because he told them he was. Laughing hard, he wondered what he'd do if the right woman came along and snatched him up. He thought that he'd still be the greatest uncle of all time because he'd make sure that he was.

Now all he had to get ready for was Christmas, and he was going to have so much fun with that holiday. He had plenty of people to buy for this year, and he'd been planning all year—well since they came into the family, a gift for each and every one of his sisters-in-law. His brothers, too, but he'd never bought for a young woman before, and he was looking forward to it.

~*~

Olivia didn't have any idea why she thought being a personal shopper the day after Thanksgiving would be a good idea. No one knew what they wanted, and it was up to her to get them to buy the biggest ticket item she could from them. The man she was working with right now didn't even know if his wife would wear a robe around the house, much less what color to get her. And since he wanted it monogrammed as well, there would be no regifting it the day after Christmas either.

" White is a good color to go with, yes. It will match any pajamas that she has." He didn't want her to have to have too many pajamas either. So when she suggested that he get her a pair of those, he balked at the idea. " How about some nice slippers. You can get those monogrammed as well."

" Now that would be nice. She'd know how much I love her with that." She didn't understand how putting her initials on something was a sign of love, but she didn't believe in love at all. She rarely believed that people loved their kids. She'd seen enough failed families—not just marriages, to last several lifetimes. " I want to get her some of that powder that you were talking about, too. The kind with the blue powder puff."

" All right." She had shown him all kinds of

powders, now all she had to do was find the one with the blue puff. She noticed a man watching the two of them and wondered what his beef was. Didn't he believe in personal shoppers? Well, she didn't either, but it paid well, and she only had to deal with one customer at a time this way. " I'll have this wrapped for you as well, correct?"

" Yes, of course." Her man was excited, and she was too. Not just to get him to the wrapping department, but to go on to the next man. They were all men that she had on her list today, and she wondered what their wives thought of the gifts that she'd convinced their husbands to buy. " Do they have monogrammed wrapping paper, too, do you suppose?"

" No, I'm sure they don't. But they have some lovely colors for you to choose from." How would that even work, she wondered as she found the blue puff. " Here you go. All finished with the wife now. Is there anything else I can help you with?"

" I'm finished shopping then. You've been a wonderful help." She nodded, distracted by the man who seemed to be following them around. " I'll tell your manager how helpful you were, and perhaps you can get a raise. Wouldn't that be nice this time of year?"

" It would." The man wasn't being too cagey about following them. He was staring at the man she was with like he owed him money. When her customer walked away, the other man came up to her and smiled. " Can I help you? I really can't, just so you know. I'm someone's personal shopper today, and I have appointments all day."

" You didn't think that the robe was a good idea." She said that was what he wanted. " Yeah, he did, I heard him turn down everything you suggested. But you didn't think the robe was a good idea. Why? I have five sisters-in-law that I was going to get one each for, but now I'm second-guessing myself."

" Have you ever seen them wearing a robe? I'm assuming that your brothers are their husbands. Do they wear robes? Who wants to put on an extra piece of clothing before they dash to the shower and take it off again? Unless you've seen them in a robe, I would assume that they don't wear them. If they get up out of bed and shower right away, they're not going to be putting on a robe. That's just my opinion. But if you want to get the five of them, did you say? Robes, then go for it. I can't help you. I have another appointment in ten minutes, and as I said, I'm booked all day."

" I'll pay you double whatever you're making from them to get you to work with me." She said that some of these people had their appointments set up since July. " I can work with that. Just name your price. I was thinking I'd get them all the same thing and be done with it, but I can see now where that would be a bad idea."

" Look, Mister. I have plenty to do without picking up another shopper. You'll have to talk to my manager and see what he has to say. But let me tell you, he's going to tell you the same thing that I did. I'm booked all day." He followed her to her break area and said he'd pay her whatever she wanted for some of her time. " I can't do that. I have to do what I've been set up to do."

When she was on her third customer of the morning, he was getting his wife a toaster and a blender for Christmas, the man came around her again. But this time he was with her manager. And he had a huge smile on his face. She just knew this wasn't going to bode well for her, and she was sort of put out that he'd done what she'd said and gone to her manager. She guided her customer to the wrapping department and walked away.

" Olivia, I'd like for you to meet Mr. Zander Erickson. He's going to have you as his personal shopper for the rest of the day." She asked about her bookings, the ones that he'd told her were important. " This gentleman is going to have you help him shop for his entire family. Children included. I'll find someone else to get with your customers today. This is important for the store."

" All right. I'll do it." But she wasn't going

to be happy for it. One shopper meant no tips, and she'd gotten a good one from numbers one and two today. " How many people do you have to buy for Mr. Erickson?"

" Twenty-two. My brothers, their wives, their children, as well as my secretary and a few other people that I have on my list. I thought that I'd just do this the easy way, and then I heard you talking to your customer and realized that buying them all the same kind of gift would be a waste of time. My brothers have never worn robes in their lives. The women might, but I don't know them well enough to get them that. And the children wouldn't think of me as their favorite uncle if I were to buy them something as lame as a robe. I have to be the favorite uncle." She asked him where he wanted to start. " My brothers. I have a good idea what to get them, but I want to make sure that it's going to be epic. I'm the only one that's not married, and I want to get them something that reminds them how much fun I'm having without a wife."

It took them nearly two hours to get the gifts for his brothers. It was going to be fun, she thought. He'd got them all a game system with different games so that he could play with them all the time. They could also play with their kids, as he'd gotten games for their ages, too.

Mr. Erickson also got a small handheld game

for his secretary so that she'd have something to do when he was stuck in court all day. She thought that was a good gift as he seemed to think that she didn't have much to do while he was gone.

At lunchtime, she was going to the cafeteria to have some lunch when he followed her. Buying her lunch was probably frowned upon, but he was funny and knew how to spend money when he wanted something. It wasn't as if she didn't know who he was; everyone knew of the Ericksons, but she doubted that few saw them as she was seeing this man today. He was having a good time, and she was catching his mood more and more as she hung out with him.

After lunch, they hit the floor for the kids. He really was going to be the favorite uncle with what he was buying the kids. There were beautiful toys for the little girl that she wished she could have afforded, and trucks for the young boys. He showed her a picture of all the kids while they were looking for the perfect gift. They were beautiful families, and he seemed to have an endless supply of pictures of them on his phone.

" Now I have to get my cook something. She's been complaining about her hips hurting for a while now and is going to retire. I would love to get her a beautiful cane that she can use when she's off working." She asked if she'd broken her hip. " Yes. And she's had a hip replacement, too. I'm going to miss her."

The canes were lovely, and she thought it thoughtful that he'd picked out something that he thought she'd use. When he had her initials engraved on the handle, so she'd not lose it, Olivia wanted to hug him. He'd put a lot of thought into her gift, and she thought it wonderful.

The rest of his staff was going to get cash, he told her. " They'll have to do with that because I don't have that much time to get them something. I would like some pretty envelopes for the cash if you have them." She showed him the money cards that they had, and he bought a dozen of them. The man was really racking up the cash in his shopping, but he said he wanted to be done today, and this was working out better than he could have imagined.

It was nearly four o'clock when they finished with everyone but the women in his life. He really did have five beautiful sisters-in-law, and he was stumped as to what to buy them. She had an idea that he wanted it to be personal, so she suggested he buy them frames and have the pictures that he'd taken yesterday put in them. There were pictures of each of his brothers with their wives and children, if they had any.

" It'll be outdated next year, but you said that this would be all of their first Christmas's together, correct?" He nodded and smiled. " I mean, I'd want to have a memory for my first holiday with my family if I had one. I don't think you could get more personalized than that, even though they're all the same gift, they'll be of their families."

" Perfect. Can I get it done here? Today?" She said that there was a photo shop in the store, but she didn't know how big he wanted them. After he told her, they then looked at the frames that he'd need. He picked out five of the most expensive ones they carried, and she thought it was going to make him the best brother-in-law ever with these gifts. " You've helped me so much. I can't believe that I'm finished. I'm doing this next year with you. You hit on everything that I needed and then some. Can I tip you?"

" Yes, you can tip me, but remember, I might not be able to do this next year. They only take a few of the staff to do this, and I just happened to be picked for this year." He said she was going to have the best day of all of them. " More than likely. You've spent a great deal of money today. But I don't know."

" I'll pull some strings." She just bet he would too, and she didn't doubt that even if she didn't get picked, she'd be his personal shopper when he came in. He'd really spent a fortune on his gifts this year and had them wrapped. The wrapping alone was going to be in the hundreds of dollars. " What time do you get off? I would love to take you out to dinner for all your help."

" You don't have to do that. I'm just working here, and you happened to get me. I'm sure that any one of the others could have gotten you what you wanted."

" Doubtful. I had a good time too, and it's not something that I do every day. Shopping for anything isn't something that I usually enjoy. This has been the best day that I've had in a while, and I think it's all thanks to you." She looked around to see if anyone was listening in on what he was saying, and was embarrassed to see her boss there. When Mr. Erickson saw him, he told him the same thing. That he'd never had this much fun shopping before. " I was just asking her to dinner because I'm finished and I'd like to celebrate with her. I know that it must be frowned upon, but I'd really like to take her out. Is that something I can do?"

" What Olivia does in her free time is totally up to her." The manager winked at her, and she nearly fell backward. He rarely, if ever, had anything good to say to his employees. And she'd never been winked at by him. " She has to finish out her day, however, and that would be getting you out the door happy. I must say, I've been keeping an eye on things with her, and she did a good job of getting you to the correct departments today."

" Yes, she did. And she steered me in the right direction, too, when I didn't have a clue what to get my family. They're going to be completely blown away by the gifts that she helped me pick out, too." They shook hands. " I'm ready to check out and she said that I can have these all delivered to my house. I'd like that service as well."

Mike was falling all over himself getting Erickson in the right direction. She could have done that, too, but it looked like she'd done her job and was now dismissed. Getting her things gathered up after clocking out, she decided that she was going to treat herself to some dinner out. She'd had a really good day today, and she deserved it.

As she was leaving the building, a long limo pulled up in front of her. She narrowly missed getting hit by the car and cursed at the driver when he tipped his hat at her. Just as she was going to go around him, he got out of the car and opened the back door. There sat Mr. Erickson with a stupid-looking grin on his face.

" Mike said you'd be getting off soon. I was afraid that I'd miss you." She said that she was headed home. " Dinner with me, please? It's been a perfect day, and I'm not finished celebrating yet. I promise you that I have no ill will with my intentions. Just dinner, then I'll make sure you get home. Besides, I didn't get to tip you yet."

She was torn about what to do. If she went out with him, there would be all kinds of things that could go wrong with it. She really could use the tip he might give her, too. But he was an Erickson who was used to getting his own way. Getting into the limo, she knew that she was going to regret this as soon as the door was closed.

Chapter 2

Zander didn't even have his tree up yet, and he was finished shopping. Except for a few gifts that he might have forgotten, he'd never been this finished before the night before Christmas. He was about as happy about that as he'd ever been. And he didn't think he'd spent all that much either when he considered that he'd bought gifts for nearly thirty people all totaled.

He kept thinking about dinner last night, too. He'd had so much fun with Olivia that he wanted to see her again. She had been the most fun because she said that she was waiting for him to pull out a knife or gun and kill her.

" That's what I get for going out with a stranger. I should listen to my head more." He asked her what her head was telling her. " That just because you spent all day with someone doesn't mean that you should be spending the evening with them as well. That's just insane."

She'd pointed out the cameras that had them being together and telling him that he'd never get away with murdering her. She was a delight all evening, and when he took her home, he couldn't believe that she wouldn't allow him to walk her to the door.

" There are bushes on either side of my door. And I have no cameras there. You could kill me and put me in the bushes, and no one would ever find me. I've told my landlord that they're overgrown, but he's like most men, he doesn't listen." He asked her if she thought that he didn't listen. " You listen all right. I bet you could tell me what the first thing you said to me. Not that it matters. But you, being a lawyer and all, you pay attention to things like that."

" I do. And I asked you how I was to get you to work for me." She nodded, and he wanted to make her laugh. " What if I promise not to kill you when I take you to the door? I swear on my niece's heart that I'd never harm you."

" I'm sure that's what every murderer would say." He laughed again. Hard and without thought of how much fun he was having about murdering someone. " You're very strange. Has anyone ever told you that before?"

" No. Not to my face anyway." She said that it was probably because of all of his money. " More than likely. I'm sure that my brothers would think I'm strange for going out with a woman who is plotting her own demise. Do you date that often? I'm betting that your job keeps you from dating too much."

" You'd be correct. I have two jobs right now.

I figured that no knight in shining armor is going to come my way, so if I want something, I'm going to have to get it for myself." He asked her what she wanted. " A home, mostly, a car that runs when I need it to and not when it's ready. Nothing much more than that."

" What about your utilities and food on the table?" She said if she could have the other two, then she felt like she'd won the lottery. " I think I know just what you're saying about that, too."

The rest of the night was like that. It was as if getting to know her was going to be something that he wanted all his life. She was brilliant and funny. Spoke her mind when she had something to say, and she apparently loved a good game of chess.

" Not that I play all that well, but I love the way your mind has to work in order to play. Not only do you have to know the moves each piece makes, but you also need to be able to think about what your opponent is going to be doing as well." He told her that he liked a good game of chess too. " Good. Chess is like being a lawyer. You have to keep your mind sharp as a lawyer, and I would imagine that you need to know what your opponent is up to, too."

" I've never been compared to a game of chess before, but I think you hit it right on the nail. Thank you for that." She nodded and got out of the car. He couldn't see her going into her place because of all the bushes. She'd been right. They really were overgrown and full of weeds, too. He was going to have to look into that before they took over the front of the apartment she was living in.

His day went better than he thought it might. He'd had such a good time last night that he found himself thinking about how much enjoyment he'd had. It wasn't often that he went out with a woman and wanted a second date. He was cautious, however. He didn't think that he was falling in love with Olivia, but he certainly had fun with her when they went out.

It was then that he realized that he didn't have her phone number or her last name. Christ, he'd surely been slacking on that. He'd just go to the store and ask her. She was more than likely working today, and he wanted to see her again anyway. Shutting down his computer, not that he was working that hard on anything, and he headed to the store he'd found her in yesterday.

She was with another customer, so he waited around until she was finished. As soon as she turned the people over to the wrapping department, he made his move. She wasn't as happy to see him as he was to see her. She looked like she was fighting something, too. Like she was in pain with something.

" I have a killer headache. You can't have figured out that you didn't buy something for someone on your list. Your things haven't even been delivered yet." He said he wanted her phone number. And her last name. " Why? You're not the usual kind of person that someone like me dates. And it can't be because you find me charming. I was rude to you last night, and you know it."

" I found you refreshing." She pointed out that she wasn't an air freshener, and he found himself laughing again. " You're fun to be around. I have no idea why I enjoy you calling me a murderer, but I do find you to be a lot of fun, and I'd like to see you again. And again if you wish."

" What I wish is that I could get rid of this headache and go home to take a nap. What is it with people wanting to buy robes for people on their list? I own one, but I can't remember a single time when I wore it. They're useless. Unless you have a baby or toddler in the house and you have to get up in the middle of the night." He suddenly saw her heavy with his child and didn't know what to make of that. He realized that he'd missed something that she'd said and asked her to repeat herself. " I said, what is it you really want. I'm not going to sleep with you. I have better things to do with my life than to be a notch on your bedpost. I'm sure you have plenty there as of now."

" You don't have a very high opinion of me, do you?" She said that she didn't know him all that well, but didn't have a very high opinion of most people. " Neither do I, for that matter. I find people to be greedy and mean. And that's saying a great deal since I have to deal with the public on a daily basis."

" Me too." She took a pen from her pocket and wrote her number down on a sheet of sticky paper that she had in another pocket. " If you don't call, then I'm going to be right about you. You're just like every other rich jerk who thinks that I can be a plaything. I won't lose any sleep over it either. My last name is Marsh. And yes, I'm related to the Marshes that you've no doubt heard from, but I have nothing to do with them."

" I don't know anyone by that name. Are you famous?" She only snorted at him. Delighted, he laughed. " I'm going to call you and have dinner with you again. I promise."

" We'll see. Just look up my family, and you'll understand why I'm currently working two jobs and trying to buy myself my own home." He promised her that he would as soon as he got home. " My next robe buyer is here, so I have to go. You have a good life, Mr. Erickson. In the event that I don't hear from you again, I want you to know that, despite not being murdered by you last night, I had a good time."

" Are you saying that you wished I'd have murdered you?" She shrugged and told him to look her up. " I'm going to. And I'm sure that it's not as bad as you think it might be."

" We'll see." She greeted her next customer with a smile that didn't reach her eyes. He had a feeling that she was going to be spending a great deal of time in the robe department today. He wondered where she got her charming attitude towards customers. He supposed that she was just good at her job.

Leaving the store, he wrote down her last name and headed home. While sitting in his car, he added her phone number and name to his phone list and was happy that she'd been nice enough to give it to him. As he was pulling into traffic, he thought about how she was so sure that he'd not want anything to do with her when he looked her up. No, he thought to himself, he couldn't see himself giving up on her when she had made him laugh so much. Perhaps it wouldn't go anywhere, but he was willing to try.

Laughing as he drove home, he thought about how she was the most standoffish person he'd ever met. She knew how to keep him at arm's length, and he was sort of happy about that. She wasn't going to be the love of his life, but he thought that he could have some fun with her until the right woman came along. If there was someone out there for him. At this point, he didn't care. He was only looking for a good time, and she could make him laugh, and he was happy with that.

It didn't take him long to get back home. The first thing he did was look up the Marsh family and found that she was from a very prestigious family. Or they had been at one time. He was sure there were many skeletons in her closet and decided to have a look. Just as it was coming up on a background check on her, he could see where her family had been in the news a great deal of late. Money laundering was the biggest scandal that came up, but there were other things as well. Like non-payment of taxes was a big one, too.

He read over the report on her parents while he was having a sandwich of bologna and cheese. It was still his favorite sandwich as an adult. He'd enjoyed this particular type of sandwich since he and Martha would share lunch together. She also introduced him to putting chips on it so that it had some crunch to it. He missed that woman more than he did his own parents. Which wasn't saying much as he'd not had anything to do with them over the last twelve plus years.

Martha had taken them in when their van had broken down in front of her house. All of them had learned the true value of money while living with her, and she'd taught them how to be gentlemen of worth. She'd also taught them that love could be freely given. He'd never felt so loved in his life until she came into their lives. He knew that he and his brothers had been lucky that they'd been able to have such a mentor in their lives.

She was one of a kind, and he missed her so much sometimes he'd find himself sobbing for her loss. She'd been the best thing that could have happened to them, and he'd love for her to still be around now so that she could see what they'd accomplished since she'd been gone.

After reading what he could find on the Marsh family, he did a deep background check on Olivia. He told himself he was only doing it so that he could have information on her when he dated her again, but it was wrong, and on so many levels, he knew it was.

There wasn't much on her that he could find. She worked hard and paid her way through life. She was right in saying that she had very little to do with her family. At eighteen, she'd moved out, and it looked as if she didn't have much to do with them after that. Her name was rarely mentioned in any newspaper articles that he found, and so far as the news articles went, she'd been wholly left out of their lives. He even knew what her credit score was, and that was great. Putting away his computer, he took his plate to the kitchen and decided that he'd been in the house long enough today and was headed to the office at three thirty. He knew there he'd get some work done without any distractions.

By the time six o'clock rolled around, he was exhausted. He'd gotten all the work he'd needed done on the cases he'd been working on and then some. His brother Knox had gotten a lot of research done on the case against the school principal, and he'd been shocked that they'd hired him at all. His background check had him hurting women who didn't do what he wanted from way back.

~*~

Olivia decided that she didn't care for being a personal shopper. There was a lot of smiling that she had to do, and she couldn't stand being fake. That's what it felt like to stand around with the same people for two hours and help them buy things that no one would ever use again. Like the man she was working with now. He thought that getting his wife a vacuum cleaner was the perfect gift.

If they had something in mind when she helped them, she didn't understand why they paid extra to have her shop with them. Sure, she could talk up a good game on what sort of things they had in mind, but she didn't understand why a man would think that a vacuum would be a good Christmas gift to his wife and jewelry to his mistress. There were a lot of men buying for both their wives and their mistresses. She didn't understand that either.

If you loved someone, why would you need a

mistress? She'd read the paper recently about a school principal who had beaten a woman nearly to death because she didn't want to be his mistress. The article went on to say that not only had his wife left him, but that he'd told the judge that he wanted her back so that having a mistress would work. Olivia didn't understand people and was glad that she didn't usually have much in the way of interaction with them, except during the holiday season.

When she was finished with her last customer, another robe man, she headed home. Checking her phone—she wasn't to have it on her person while she was working—she found that she'd had three messages from Mr. Erickson and two from her mother. Wondering what either of them wanted, she decided to wait until she got home before she messaged them back. When she got to her place, there were four men outside her place trimming the bushes that were at least six or seven feet tall.

" What's going on?" He said that they'd had a complaint about the bushes being an eyesore. " I called every day for a month to get them trimmed because they're dangerous for people coming and going, and someone complains about them being ugly, and that brings you out? I should have said that, I guess." She left them to their work.

Getting inside, she had gotten another message

from her mother. Texting her back, she told her she was home now if she wanted to call. Before she hit send, she let Mr. Erickson know that she would talk to him later, as her mother had called. It was only a matter of minutes before her mother called her. Something must be wrong if she was calling that fast, she thought.

" I'm leaving your father." Rolling her eyes, she asked her what he'd done this time. " I had my credit cards denied today, and it embarrassed me. I don't like to be embarrassed, Olivia. You know that."

" Yes, I learned that the hard way. It's why I don't come around anymore. You do understand that you're in trouble with the Federal Government, don't you? I don't believe Dad had anything to do with your cards being cut off. The government more than likely did that."

" Well, what did I do that would have them doing such a thing to me? I was at lunch with the girls, and someone had to pay for my meal. I'm going to be gossip fodder for the rest of the month if you don't help me leave your father." She asked what she was supposed to do. " I don't know, but you should want this for me. I'm your mother."

" You're only my mother when you need something. Remember how I embarrassed you at the club by being my age when they asked you who I was? How was I supposed to know that you didn't tell anyone that you had a grown daughter? Not that it matters anyway. You've punished me enough with that one." She asked her how she'd punished her. " You sent your goons after me, and they beat me to shit. I had to spend six hours in the emergency department that night, and I still have hurts from it."

" Oh yes, I remember now. And they're not goons but people I employ to get what I want done." She told her that was a goon. " It is not. Now behave and tell me what you're going to do about your father. He's in trouble with the IRS, and that has nothing to do with me."

" Don't you live in the same house as him?" She asked what that had to do with anything. " I'm sure that the IRS thinks that whatever happens with dad happens to you, too. You'll have to dip into your stash if you have one to make ends meet until this is over."

" I don't know what you're talking about. What do I need to have for a stash?" She rolled her eyes hard enough that she was sure that her mother knew what she was doing. " And don't use that tone with me, young lady. I'm still your mother, and what I say goes. When are you coming home to have a talk with your father?"

" Never. Why would anything I have to say to either of you have any bearing on what you're going through? As I've said to you before, you've made your choices, so you have to live with the consequences. I haven't had anything to do with you other than these calls since I left home eight years ago. I don't even know why you'd call me when you're having trouble with Dad. I never do what you want about him."

" Yes, and I'm getting sick of that as well." She sat down at her kitchen table and went through her mail while her mother went on about how she was going to send someone to pick her up. " You'll be here for dinner, or I'll send someone for you to bring you here. I'm sick of us not being a normal family."

" We've never been normal. Why should we try that now?" She dumped her junk mail in the trash can and looked at her phone. There was a message from Erickson, and she wondered if he had a mother like she did. She'd feel sorry for him if he did. " Mother, I'm busy here, and I have to get ready for work tomorrow. I'm not going there for any reason, and you should understand that by now. You and Dad have to get yourself out of whatever mess you've made and leave me out of it. I pay my taxes on time and even get a refund once in a while. You two need to budget better."

She would have hung up on her mother, but that would get her hurt. Just as she was sputtering about family and the normal way they do things, she decided that she was going to block her number and be done with her. These calls were something that she didn't look forward to, and she didn't much care for either of them.

Her parents were going to prison if she didn't miss her bet, and she was going to be happy that they were gone. They'd been nothing but trouble since she had been born, and she didn't want to deal with them anymore. Perhaps that was harsh, she told herself, but they'd been nothing but trouble for her for too long. She just wanted normal, as her mother wanted them to be.

With another threat of hurting her, her mother finally got off the phone. There were threats made of her sending her people after her, but she knew that her mother had no idea where she lived. She'd kept that out of the calls for so long that sometimes she had to remember that herself. Mother wasn't going to play fair, and she knew that. Her dad wouldn't either, but he hadn't called her yet, complaining about what was going on with him. He would, of this she had no doubt, but not right now. Answering Erickson, she decided that since he used her first name, she'd do the same to him. Now if she could only remember what it was.

Messaging that she was finally off the phone, he called her right away. He must have put her number in his phone because he had no trouble calling her back in seconds. When he started laughing, she wanted to hang up. But he made her laugh at herself, and she was willing to put up with most anything to feel as good as she had last night with him.

" I looked up your family. Your parents are in a great deal of trouble." She said that she knew that and asked him if he'd done a background check on her. " I did. Only because your name came up so few times in the articles about them, I wondered if you'd given me your name or not."

" I don't lie. I don't even like to bend the truth a little. Mother is leaving Dad again over being embarrassed about her credit card being cut up in front of her. I wish I could have been there. It would have had me laughing for decades. What did you want?" He told her that he wanted to see her again. " Wasn't last night enough for you? I mean, you already pointed out that I'm not in awe of you."

" I find that I don't care if you're in awe with me or not. You're fun to be around, and I enjoyed myself last night. I hope that you had a good time too." She told him that despite it being him she was out with, she had a good time. That, of course, made him laugh. " You should see some improvements on your bushes out front today or tomorrow. I had no idea that I owned that building until I went over my records. I didn't know things like that had been ignored."

" They were working on them when I got

home." She looked out the window and could still see the truck out front. " Had I known you owned the building, I would have told you of other things that need fixing up. Did you know that the entire building is in code violation, with the fire escapes not working? Not to mention, I think you should know that I think the landlord is jacking up the rent on people that he wants out. I've been here longer than him, and he doesn't mess with me."

" I'm making notes now." Rolling her eyes again, she wondered how long it would be before he got around to fixing even the simplest of things. But he did get the bushes trimmed back. She wondered too if he had any idea that most of the apartments were empty right now and figured that it was none of her concern. " Since I'll be able to see you, how about if I pick you up for dinner tonight. We can have some steaks and whatever you want."

" I like steaks. I can't afford them, but I like them all right." She sat down again in her kitchen chair. " What is it about me that has you wanting to go out with me again? I'm not all that pretty. I have red hair and blue eyes. Nothing much is going on with my body either. So what is it?" He thought about her.

" I think that you're beautiful. As for your red hair, I think that it shines in the daylight and simmers at night. It's comparable to the sunsetting for me. Your body is well-toned from what I can see. You don't seem to have any tattoos, but if you have any, I'd love to see them and know why you got them. You don't wear makeup for whatever reason, and I think that makes you refreshing and lovely. I could go on, but I think you understand that's not the reason that I've asked you out again." She said she didn't know. " You're smart, witty, and funny. I love that you make fun of yourself and me while you're at it. You seem to have a good sense of humor. I've noticed that you use it on me, too. I think dating you is going to be fun. It'll never be dull around you because you bring your own kind of humor to the date."

" You're certifiable." He laughed. She wondered if he had very little to laugh about in his life and asked him that. " You have to have a dull life if you think that my bashing you is funny. However, you must know that with my parents, the way that they are, that dating a lawyer isn't going to bode well for either of us. They'll think I'm out to get them. They usually do anyway."

" We're two consenting adults, one of whom just so happens to be an attorney. I won't hold what you are against you, you shouldn't me." She told him it wasn't her that he should be worried about. " I'm not afraid of your parents. I'm an attorney of good standing, and whatever they have against my kind is up to them. I've done nothing wrong."

" No, but you see, they dislike me a great deal, and if you and I see each other, then it's going to bring you down to my level, according to them. I don't want you hurt or your practice. I'm sure that you can understand that." He said he'd be just fine. " If you say so. But don't say that I didn't warn you. They're not the nicest people in the world, and they don't play fairly. In fact, the reason they're in so much trouble now is that they think that they can throw money at something and it'll go away. The problem now is they don't have the funds to toss at anything. Even the staff have left them for paying gigs."

" As I said, I can handle them. I'd love to see you tonight if that's all right with you. And we'll have a nice dinner, and I'll walk you to the door. It's cost me a lot to be able to do that." She grinned, knowing that he couldn't see her. " What do you say, Olivia? Dinner with me at a nice steak house?"

" All right, but don't say I didn't warn you." She had done all she could with him, and really, she did want to see him again. He was a lot of fun and seemed to have all his ducks in a row. " I'll see you around six. You know where I live. By the way, since this is our second date, what's your first name?"

Chapter 3

Caroline had to look twice to make sure that it was her daughter with a man on her arm. Getting up out of her seat, she made her way toward where she'd seen her and lost them in the crowd. She'd better not be dating that man. If she had it right, his name was Knox Erickson, and he had been hired as her attorney. Caroline couldn't find them anywhere. Hubert asked her what she was doing.

" I thought that I saw Olivia with that Erickson man. The one that you said would make us a great attorney. He turned us down, didn't he?" He said that he couldn't afford him. " Same thing. And who said that we couldn't afford him? Did he say that to you?"

" He works for his family and nothing more. He told me that his contract was with the family, and if we were to want him to break that, it would cost us the price of his contract with them. He's the best there is. If Olivia is dating him, then you can be assured that she's into something about us with him. For all I know, he's on the other side of the desk from us when we go to court." Caroline said that he'd better not be. " I don't know. Just leave them alone. I'll get to the bottom of it tomorrow. My sister is taking us out to eat, so let's not talk about court hearings or unpaid taxes. I just want to have a good meal on her dime."

" She should be bailing us out, is what she should be doing." Hubert said that she didn't have that kind of money. " She should give us what she has so we can leave the country then. I've had it with taxes and the like. And now they're saying that you've been doing some money laundering for the mob. I never heard the likes of that before."

" Look. There she is. Let's just have a nice dinner and be done with it. Mae said that the only way she was going to dine with us was if we didn't mention our woes. Remember that when you decide to bring up the stuff with the house." Caroline huffed and told her husband that she would bring up what she wanted. " Then we'll be stuck with the bill, and I know for a fact that we don't have any charging power left on any of our credit cards. Do you want to wash dishes here tonight to pay for our meal? I certainly don't. And Mae will leave us high and dry. You know she won't take any shit from either of us."

" I wish every day that I had not married you. You've been nothing but trouble since we got back from our honeymoon." He told her that he felt the same way, but they were in too deep right now to care about things that happened over fifty years ago. " I just want it out there that I would divorce you had I the forethought to do it before now. Now, as you said, we're stuck together. Hello Mae. It's nice of you to invite us to dinner tonight."

" Hello, Caroline. Still bringing up the past like you can change it, are you? Well, I won't have my birthday dinner ruined because you two don't have any idea how to live within your means. I don't want to hear about it." They were seated, and she had a thought that they'd not gotten her anything for her birthday. Not that it mattered, she wouldn't like anything that they got for her anyway.

" How long are you in town for? And where are you staying? Not with us, I presume." Caroline took her seat and was pleased when a young man pushed her chair in for her. " I've missed being taken care of when we go out, Hubert. We need to get things back on track so that we can have this kind of perks."

" You have that right. That house is falling down around your ears. Why you still live in it is beyond comprehension. You should get yourself something smaller, like I did. I have two bedrooms and a kitchen, and I find that's all I need. Cuts down on the heating bill too." Hubert said that they could only afford the house that they were in. " Oh yes. Money troubles. I try not to remember that. You should have paid your taxes, and that's all I'm going to say about that."

Caroline had always hated Mae Simpleton. Even before her husband died, she'd always thought of her as a simpleton. She could never say that to his face, as he was a mean man and would take advantage of any situation that they were in. Like ten years ago, when he'd realized that they weren't paying their taxes back then, he'd reported them to the IRS. It had taken everything they owned to get out of that mess, and now he'd done it again. Or at least she thought he had. It would have been something that he would have done to them if he hadn't been dead for the last five years or so.

" Where is Olivia? I thought I had made it clear that I wanted her here with us, too. She's the only one of the three of you who makes me laugh. You two are always into something that is on the wrong side of the law, and that depresses me." Hubert said that she could help them out if she wished. " I don't wish it. I have a full life in front of me, and I don't want to give you all my hard-earned money so that in another five years or so you can be right where you are. Besides, it's not like you have any intentions of paying me back. Do you?"

" We don't have a pot to piss in. Is that what you wanted to hear? And once the IRS gets finished with us this time, we won't even have the house anymore. I don't know what they expect us to do without any place to live. Go live with Olivia, I suppose." She shuddered to think about that and looked at her husband. " I don't even know where she lives nowadays, do you? She just goes about her business like she has nothing to do with us. I think that she should be in as much trouble as we are, but not to hear her talk about it. She thinks she's distanced herself enough from us that she doesn't need us."

" She doesn't need you. Last I heard, she was a full-grown woman who has a job and pays her taxes. She's even got enough money each month to put some away. Not a lot, but some money that she's been saving for a house." She'd not known that and was wondering how she could get it from Olivia. Whatever it was, it would be something more than they had now. While she was trying to calculate how much there might be and what she could use it for, damned if she didn't show up at their table. " Look, she at least remembered my birthday, other than expecting me to pay for her meal with some man. Look how beautiful she looks right now."

" Aunt Mae. Father, Mother. I thought that I saw you three when we got here. Everyone, this is Zander. Zander, this is my parents and my Aunt Mae on my father's side. It's her birthday today." He shook Hubert's hand, and she just stared at it when he put it to her. " Mother, don't be a bitch. He was just saying hello to you. There is no reason for you to act like this with him."

" I know you. You turned us down as our attorney." He said that he'd not, he'd remember that if that had happened. " Then you have a brother or something that's an attorney. He said that we couldn't afford him."

" That may well be true. If he were to work outside the family, then he'd have to break his contract. That would be costly and no reason for him to do that." She huffed at him and looked at her husband while he continued. " I'm an attorney as well. My brother and I work on cases together, but sometimes he has to field calls that would take us away from the family. I hope you understand."

" I don't. If someone wants to hire you, then you should be hired." That made more sense in her head, but it pissed her off that she'd messed up. " I don't care for anyone telling me no. And that would include my daughter. I told her not to date, and here she is flaunting it right in my face."

" You told me not to date men who were related to your friends. Since I know for a fact that you don't have any friends, that leaves the field wide open for me. Mother, your temper is showing, and I know how much Aunt Mae hates that." Olivia looked at her aunt. " I just wanted to say happy birthday, Aunt Mae. And

I hope to see you around while you're visiting. How long do you plan to stay?"

" I'm leaving on Friday, a week from today. I have things that I must see to before I can go on that cruise that I've been thinking about. I'm going to see Europe. Won't that be fun? You should come with me. Bring your young man with you." She kissed her on the cheek and told her that it wasn't possible. Caroline wondered why she never invited her on any of her trips and realized it was because they didn't like each other. " We'll have to plan something soon, my dear child. Something that we can all enjoy while your parents are wallowing in their woes."

" For someone who didn't want to bring up our woes, as you call them, you sure are bringing them up a great deal. What's that all about?" Mae said that it was her birthday and she was able to pick the topics that she wished. " So long as they're about us and what's happening with your only brother. Is that right?"

" It is. I'm glad that you're catching on." Instead of getting into a shouting match with Mae, she slapped her daughter. It usually gave her a nice little buzz when she did something like that, knowing that she wouldn't retaliate no matter where they were. But it was the man who was with her that scared her a bit. The look on his face meant something more than she thought that she could handle right now. Anger like she'd never seen before. " I'm glad that you've shown yourself, Caroline. Dinner is over for the two of you. Get out before I call the police and have you trespassed. You've barked up the wrong tree."

They had a little trouble leaving the table. They'd drawn quite a crowd of people with their phones out, recording them. Embarrassed beyond anything that she'd ever felt before, Caroline decided that she was going to get back at Olivia and soon. The blood on her lip gave her a brief satisfaction, but it was short-lived when Olivia and Erickson sat down at the table they were being shown away from.

" You'll regret this, Olivia. I promise you that you will." She said that she already regretted being her child and that was going to end soon. " What do you think you can do about it? Nothing, that's what. And don't think that you can have your little stash of money and me not get it. I'm going to go to the bank tomorrow and get it all out and leave you homeless. I'm sick of you acting so superior to us. We're your parents."

" So it says on my birth certificate. But that doesn't mean shit where I'm concerned. And you go ahead and try to get to my money at the bank. I've learned my lesson the last time that you did that." She asked her what she thinks she could do to keep her from it. " You'll see as soon as you try. I'm not as stupid as you think I am. I've learned from the best, and I'm not going to allow you to rule me again."

" We'll just see about that." Standing up, she hated that the man, the Erickson man, was so much taller than her. It bothered her when people couldn't look up to her, and this was no different. " Come on, Hubert. I'm suddenly not hungry. We'll go home and have a nice dinner like we usually do."

" There is no staff, so I have no idea what you think is going to happen. Olivia, you have a nice evening, and watch out for your mother. She's on the warpath again." Caroline wanted to hit Hubert, but he'd hit her back, and she didn't have time to get into it with him. As they were leaving the restaurant, they were resetting the table for the three of them, and she felt her eye twitch when her anger got the better of her.

" Mrs. Marsh, please don't return to this establishment again. I will have you arrested if you do." She just stared at the man at the front desk at the doorway. " We all know your face now, and so to save you any more embarrassment, don't come here again. I will have you arrested."

" I wouldn't come back here if you paid me to eat here. I'm going to give you a bad review too, see that I don't." He said he wasn't worried about her. Which was right on her part. She didn't have a clue how to use a computer, much less leave a review for someone. " You'll regret this. See that you don't. I'm going to own you by this time tomorrow."

" As I said, I'm not worried about you. Have the life you deserve, and like I've said to you several times, don't return. Not even if you could prove that you could afford to eat here, I will have the police come by and take you out in cuffs." She was being shoved out the door by Hubert and was pissed at him. As they were getting into their car, not even a limo could they afford to look good, she sat on her side of the car and fumed. Her eye was twitching again, and it pained her in the head. Damn it all to fuck and back, this wasn't the way she wanted to spend the evening.

" Well, I hope you're happy. I was going to see if I could get Mae to lend us some money so that we could afford a real attorney. But you had to go and piss her off." She said that she was pissed off, too, and asked him if that mattered. " You're forever pissed off, so now is no different. As soon as we get home, I want you to get in touch with Mae and tell her how sorry you are. Otherwise, she and Olivia are going to gang up against us, and we'll have no one in our corner. We can't even get our daughter to give us money now. Don't you understand how to butter someone up? Christ, this is so fucked up that I don't know if we'll ever see the light of day. I'm too old to go to prison, Caroline. So are you. We'll never make it on the inside, and that's the truth."

" Then we'll have to hope that Olivia has enough money to get us a good attorney." She wished that she could get the Erickson man to work for them, but she'd burnt that bridge. " Maybe she'll marry him, and we'll have the money that we need. He's supposed to be rich. Do you suppose that if he became our son-in-law, he'll be more receptive to helping us?"

He just snorted and drove them home. There was nothing there to eat, and she was suddenly starving. They didn't even have the money to stop at a burger place, as much as she hated to eat there, and that was all Olivia's fault. The damned girl should know better than to cross her.

~*~

Zander didn't know what to think right now. They were having a good time with her Aunt Mae, but he had a feeling that she was hurting not just from the slap that her mother had given her, but that he'd witnessed the entire thing. He wanted to reassure her that he was used to that kind of thing, but had a feeling that wouldn't go over all that well. He decided to tell her about his family as soon as they were alone. It might not help, but he wanted her to know that he knew what abuse felt like. When she got up to use the bathroom, he watched her walk away. His heart really did hurt for her.

" Young man, what are your intentions with my niece?" He said that they were just having a good time dating right now. " You look at her like she's the world to you. Are you in love with her?"

" No. I'm just dating a woman who makes me laugh. And she does too. A great deal about myself as well." Mae said that she was covering up for something. " I'm beginning to see that. I think that until now, I didn't know what to make of her parents. They're not all that loving, are they?"

" They only had her because of a mistake. If she'd been on top of things like I think she might well have been, she'd have aborted my niece right away. But I think she figured that she'd never get pregnant because she didn't want to. She's a fool." He nodded and asked her what her intentions were about Olivia. " Leave her with all that I have. She's the only family that I love, and I do love her. So if you have any intentions of hurting her, all the money you have will mean nothing if I have to come after you."

" I have no intentions of hurting her at all. We're only going out to have a good time. This is only our second date." She nodded and looked in the direction that Olivia had gone. " You love her very much, don't you?"

" I do. She's everything that I ever hoped for in a child. And to be saddled with her parents has only made her better. They say that you are what you're raised to be, and I believe that to be as true as it could be for her." She looked at him. " You'll have to watch them. For her, too. They'll come after her."

" I get that feeling as well. What do you know about her money? She told me that she's saving for a home." She said it was the first she'd heard of it tonight. " I have a feeling that she'll make sure that they can't get into her accounts. I wouldn't put it past Caroline to try, though. She's determined to hurt her daughter."

" Hubert will as well. Tonight was a better night for him, though I don't trust him as far as I can throw him. He's just like his wife in that they'll do what is necessary to get out from under going to jail. I think they'll be lucky if they don't go to prison for what they've been doing. Neither one of them could save a dime if they were forced to. They still spend it like they have it."

" I looked into their case. They don't stand a chance of keeping themselves out of jail. For how long is the question. I'd go for all I could get, but then I'm not prosecuting them." She threw back her head and laughed. Like her niece, she found humor in the strangest things. " Olivia is a great deal like you. I'm surprised that you're different from what I thought you'd be."

" I distanced myself from them as soon as I could. I've been keeping an eye on them as well. I know that Caroline hires some men to go after Olivia when she thinks about her. I don't think that's all that often, but when she does, it doesn't bode well for our girl." Olivia joined them at the table again, and he could see that she'd been crying. " Are you going to let them get the better of you, or are you going to fight back? The Olivia that I know wouldn't allow them to do what Caroline did to you today."

" I'm happy to say that I'm going to fight back. I should have when you told me to a long time ago. But I thought they'd come around to loving me. I can see now that that's not going to happen. Why they had me…well, it matters little now. But I'm going to take action against them as soon as tomorrow. I'm sick of being their whipping dog." She looked at him. " I told you that you'd not want to date me anymore, and I was right. It's all right. I understand. You have a good life, and there is no point in fucking it up by hanging around with me."

" I love having fun with you. And I'm not worried about them. You should, however. They're out to get you, and I worry for your safety." She told him about how her mother had some goons who would find her. " Goons? You actually call them that to her face?"

" She said they were just people that she hires to do what she wants. I know the definition of goon and that's more or less what it says. People that you hire to do your dirty work. And I guess keeping me in line is considered that. I wish I had the resources to make sure that they went to prison. I'd be thrilled to death to have them behind bars. My luck, they'll get out and terrorize me anyway." She looked away, but not before he saw the tears in her eyes. " You should date someone else. This has been fun, but I'm afraid of getting you hurt, and they will simply because you told them no. Even though they don't have anything close to being wealthy, they still act like they have unlimited resources. I wonder what power they have over people to get them to do what they want."

" It could be anything. Or the promise of something that the other people might think they have. I would, if I were you, call the bank in the morning and tell them that you will not tolerate them allowing anyone into your account." She said she'd done that in the bathroom. " Good for you. See? I told you that you were brilliant. I wish that I could help you out with them, but I wouldn't even know where to begin."

" Lock them up and throw away the key?" Caroline ordered for the table, and he was fine with that. He worried that Olivia wouldn't eat, and she had only just told him that she was starving before they came to tell her aunt happy birthday. A lot had changed in the few minutes since then. " I'm going to enjoy myself. So far, this has turned out to be a shitty birthday, but it's getting better. Young man, you have to tell me about your family. I've read all about you six, and I'm wondering where you've been all your life."

He told her about them moving to Tennessee from Ohio and how they'd broken down right in front of Martha Garbles home. Then how they had stayed with her for a time in order to learn all they could from her.

" She was the best thing that happened to us. Not only did she help us out when we needed it, but she made sure that we were good men too. When she died, it was the saddest day of our lives. But she'd been sickly, and her dying ended her suffering. But I miss her every day and wish she were still around." Mae said that she knew Martha from meetings that they used to go to together. " She didn't go too much after we moved in. We were busy getting the house set up for her. My oldest brother went to nursing school while she was getting around because we knew she wasn't going to be around forever. And it helped her die at home like she wanted. She was the best person in the world."

" That she was. And I miss her as well." They were served their salads, and he noticed that Olivia played with hers more than eating it. He understood why, but he didn't like it. He worried about her. " Olivia, my child, eat up. You're going to need your strength if you're going to be tangling with your mother's goons. I so love that word. I wonder if Caroline has any idea how stupid she sounds when she spouts off things like she did tonight."

They mostly talked about Mae's upcoming vacation. She was going on a month-long cruise around Europe and have some fun. She told him that she did something like this yearly, but this was her favorite thing to do. Get on a ship and not worry about anything but having fun.

" You should go with your aunt, Olivia. You'd be safer, and I'd not have to worry about you. Also, out on the seas, you might be able to get that tan you were telling me about." She snorted at him and told him that she was going to quit doing that. She'd not realized that her parents did the same thing. " Let's not talk about them. Let's have a nice dinner and then go get an ice cream at the shop down the way from here."

" I love ice cream, as you well know." He did know that about Olivia and loved the fact that, like him, she preferred vanilla over any other flavor. " I've had a rough day today. I want a double scoop."

Without talking about her parents, dinner ended on a good note. He was still worried about her and wanted her to live with him until her parents' trial. But he didn't want her to tell him no when he was just getting to know her. Zander thought that he was getting in over his head and worried about that, too. He wasn't ready to fall in love with the woman just yet, and he could feel himself slipping in that direction. Falling in love with Olivia could be a good thing or a bad thing, and he hadn't decided on which yet.

After dinner, they had ice cream. As she requested, Olivia had a double scoop of vanilla, as did her aunt. They could pass as daughter and mother; they were so much alike. The same sense of humor, too, was there. He wondered how much time Olivia had spent with her aunt while growing up and thought it must have been a good amount. They even finished each other's sentences; they were so close.

After dropping Olivia off at her apartment, she still wouldn't hear of him walking her to the door. He made sure she got in before he went to his own home. He had plenty of work to do still, as it was only nine in the evening. Pulling up his computer to see what he could get into, he got a notification that his presents would be delivered tomorrow. He decided that instead of working, he was going to put up his tree. It would make the house more festive anyway.

It took him until nearly three in the morning to get it set up and decorated. It looked great if he did say so himself. Zander knew that his other brothers had put theirs up the day after Thanksgiving, and he was happy that he'd gotten his done in plenty of time. Now, if one of them came over, they wouldn't tease him about not being in the mood. It probably would take him longer to take the tree down, but for now, he was thrilled that he'd gotten it done.

Dragging himself up to bed, he nearly got in without changing. Not that he wore anything to bed, but he didn't want to sleep in his clothes either. As he realized that he had glitter all over him, he decided to take a shower. After getting out, he was so tired that he didn't think he was going to make it to bed. Just as he was setting his alarm on his phone to get up by nine, he realized that most of his evening had been spent thinking about Olivia. Tomorrow, he was going to make sure that he hired a couple of people to follow her around. He didn't want anything to happen to her, not on his watch.

Rolling to his back, he gave himself a good talking to about falling in love. He really wasn't ready for it and hoped that Olivia felt the same. Laughing, he thought to himself if she was feeling herself falling in love with him, she'd tell him. She wasn't shy about telling him how things were going. That was one of the many things that he liked about her. Her ability to tell him straight up how she was feeling.

Chapter 4

Today was no different than any other day at work. Olivia had more customers than she'd had on the first day. Of course, she'd lost them all because her boss had assigned her to Zander all day, but she was willing to forgive him for that. He was fun to be around, and she thought that he was about as nice to her as her parents were mean.

She'd heard from the bank that someone was trying to get into her accounts. Her mother was demanding that she turn it all over to her, and that wasn't going to happen. The bank manager said that she'd told them that she had permission, but they still had to check. She'd heard that her mother had thrown a fit because they didn't believe her, and that nearly got her arrested. She wished that it had. That would have made her day.

Her dad had left her two messages last night. Olivia hadn't listened to them until this morning, but it was more of the same. He wanted her to hand over her money so that they could eat. They were sick of having cereal, all they knew how to fix, and it was her responsibility to make sure that they were getting enough to eat. She wasn't sure how that was her responsibility, but she didn't get back with him anyway.

" Miss, I'd like to see what you have in kitchenware. My wife was telling me that she needs a new juicer. I didn't know that we had one, but she insisted that she's had it for some time now. What do you have?" Taking the man to the kitchen department, she showed him all the items that they had there.

The layout of kitchen items matched one another, and when she tried to get him to get something else, other than a juicer. He said he knew what she wanted and was going to stick with that. Some people didn't have much in the way of imagination.

As she went through her day, she encountered several people like the man from this morning. They knew just what they wanted to get their wives, and her suggestions were not useful. She wanted to ask them why they were coming to her if they were so certain, but she didn't. At least she wasn't running a cash register right now, and that looked to be a good thing. They were busy out the ass, and she wanted no part of it.

After lunch, missing talking to Zander, she finished off her sandwich and was headed to the bathroom when her cell phone rang. She wasn't allowed to have it on the floor, but she could take it on break with her. Playing a game would relax her while she helped with shopping, and she was getting good at matching all the little gems. She saw that the number was Zander's and almost didn't answer. But in the end, she did.

" I thought that you'd have enough of me and my family and wouldn't call anymore." He said that he wasn't dating her family. " You shouldn't be dating me. Haven't I proved to you that I'm more trouble than I'm worth?"

" I enjoy our time together. I have a request. My brother is having us over for dinner tonight, and I was wondering if you'd go with me. It's not like I'm introducing you to my family or anything, but I thought you'd enjoy it." She told him she had a date with her aunt. " Well, that's even better. You should spend as much time with her as you can. I've learned that people you love aren't going to be around forever, and you should take every opportunity to spend time with them as you can."

" Are you telling me to do that because she's old?" He laughed and said basically that's what he was saying, but in a nicer way. " Nice or not, that's what I'm doing it for. When she called me this morning, she said that she didn't have that many years left, so I should spend her waning years with her. I told her that I'd be happy to be there with her. She and I are going to talk business. I'm not sure what that means to me from her, but I do love spending time with her."

" I'll be at my brother's if you need anything. You have my cell phone number, right?" She told him that she had it under *pain in the ass*. " I don't know why you're so mean to me. I'm the best thing that has happened to you in a while."

" You're very full of yourself this afternoon. What's gotten into you?" He told her that he got his tree up. " Wonderful. I'm sure that it'll look great with all your gifts under it. When is your stuff coming?"

" Today, between three and five. So I'm waiting around my house, getting nothing done but waiting on the van to pull up. I wonder if it will take a couple of van loads. I did go a bit overboard." She pointed out that he had to be the best uncle. " You got that right. Did I tell you that two of my sisters-in-law are going to have babies? I hope they're all little girls. We have enough men in this family as it is."

" I have to get back to work. I'm sorry that I can't see you tonight. You've become like a bad habit, and I'm going to miss you." He told her that it was sweet, and she felt her cheeks heat up. " I'll talk to you later. Try not to trip over your own ego. It might send you to the hospital."

He was still laughing when she hung up on him. She had to admit that she did have a better outlook on things once she was off the phone with him. He seemed to bring out the meanness in her, too, but he seemed to enjoy it so that was all right, she supposed.

After lunch, she didn't have a single man who wanted to see robes or kitchenware. She enjoyed helping them find the perfect gift for their wives, and she also enjoyed the way that they would look at her for advice. That's what she was there for, and she wanted to help. She was on her last customer of the day when she realized that she'd not be seeing Zander tonight. It sort of depressed her that he wasn't going to be around. But she was spending the evening with her aunt, and that would be fun as well. Aunt Mae was someone she could talk to, too, about anything.

After getting home, she checked her voicemail and found that her mother had finally gotten around to messaging her. It was about the bank notifying her that she wasn't to get into her account, and she loved that. Not that she had a great deal in her account, she kept it all in a safety deposit box, but the thought of what would happen if she were to drain her checking account would eat her up in bounced check charges.

Since neither of her parents knew where she lived, she was happy about them not finding her. The threat from her mom was bad enough, but her dad said he was going to kill her for the insurance money if she didn't help them out.

She did wonder if that was true, that they'd taken a policy out on her so they could collect on it when she was dead. But they'd had to have kept up with the payments, and she doubted that it would go all that far. She thought about telling them that just because you have a policy on her, doesn't mean you can collect on it if they didn't make any payments.

Driving to the hotel where her aunt was staying, she enjoyed the crisp weather of the evening and was sure that tomorrow they'd have snow. It would put people in a better mood when shopping, she'd learned, and might well be in a better mood herself. She loved the snowy weather but didn't much care for driving in it.

Her aunt took her to the hotel dining room, and they had a nice dinner. She'd not expected her to want to eat in the place; it was sort of run-down and not without much in the way of atmosphere. But the food was really good, and they enjoyed themselves by having nearly the entire dining room to themselves.

" I have some things I'd like to talk over with you. Now, don't tell me no. It's a done deal, and I can't think of anyone I'd rather leave my money to than you." She asked her how much there was. " Right to the point of the matter as usual. I'm worth over three million dollars. More if you count the houses that I own. I have three of those that I rent out. Plus, the one that I'm living in back home. You'll get it all."

" I suppose if I told you not to leave it to me but some charity, you'd tell me no." She said that was right. " I love you, Aunt Mae, but I'd rather have you around than your money. I know I can't stop you aging, but I'm going to miss you when you're gone."

" I'm not gone yet, so don't say that. I'll miss you too, but as I said, there is no one that I'd rather leave it to than you. Especially not your father and mother." She told her that she would think there was something wrong with her if she did that. " Quite right. I have all my marbles just where I like them, and the will is made out. I know that we don't get to see one another as much as we did when you were younger, but with your parents around, I have to be careful as well."

" I know. They'll hurt you in a heartbeat if they knew that you had that much money. More than likely kill you." She told her about the insurance policy that her dad mentioned. " I'm not worried about that so much as I am them killing me for it. I believe they will before they figure out they can't cash in a policy without making payments on it."

" Oh, darling, how did you get stuck with such parents? I just don't understand how they can be like they are. They have no reason to treat you like they have been all these years." She said she didn't know either. " I'm so sorry. I should have knocked around your father more when he was a kid. He was just like he is now. Forever thinking that whatever other people had should have been his. My mother was like that as well. Father wasn't. He just rolled his eyes and walked away when she got into one of her fits. I'm blaming your father's actions on her. Caroline is no better. The two of them are suited for one another, I believe."

" You have no idea." They finished their dinner and sat talking at the table. There were no people around them, so they enjoyed talking about whatever they wanted. Then her aunt brought up Zander and asked her what she was going to do about falling in love with the man. " We're just having fun together. That's all. He got me to help him with his shopping after Thanksgiving, and we sort of hit it off. I know better than to fall in love with him. He's not the kind of man who dates personal shoppers and marries them."

" Oh, pee shaw. He is the perfect man for you. And I'd like to know why he wouldn't think so too if that were the case. But I think he's about in love with you anyway. And why not? You're wonderful. And the perfect person for him." She said they were just friends. " Friends first is the way it works the best. You two will, if he has any sense, have a wonderful life together. Mark my words. By Christmas, you'll be so in love with him that you won't remember a time when he wasn't a part of your life. See that I'm right.

That's the way it was with your Uncle Thomas. I knew the first time that we saw each other, he was the man that I wanted to spend the rest of my life with. Then his life was cut short, and I've been lonely ever since. But for you, my dear."

When Aunt Mae cried a little, it hurt her heart too. Her uncle had been gone since before she'd been born, and she didn't know him but for the stories that she'd hear about him from her aunt. She knew that she would have loved him, and she wished that she could have gotten to know him. He must have been special because of the way that Aunt Mae still missed him after all this time.

When the time got away from them, Aunt Mae said that she needed her rest. She was normally in bed by nine-thirty, and here it was going on eleven. Walking her to her room, she hugged and kissed her aunt and asked if they were going to get together again before she left. Of course, she tried to talk her into going on the cruise with her, and she had to turn her down once again. She needed to work, and that was the way it goes at times.

Driving home, she was happy to know that her apartment would be nice and warm. It had turned cold out, and there was the threat of more snow. As soon as she pulled into her parking space, she thought something had happened.

The neighbor next door to her had had a heart attack and was headed to the hospital. They were good friends, the three of them, his wife included, and she hoped that he'd be all right. They were a nice couple, and she thought that they would die without the other one around to bicker at. They were cute in that they would argue about everything, but nothing could come between them. Just as she was getting into her place, she saw the man she'd noticed at the hotel and wondered if he was following her. Not scared at all, if he was, she confronted him on the front steps to her home.

" Mr. Erickson had us make sure you get back and forth all right." She said that she was capable of getting back and forth anywhere she went. " Yes, ma'am. I know that, but your parents know about the hotel you were at tonight, and we caught them there. They said they were only looking for you, but we had a feeling that they were up to no good."

" They were at the hotel?" He said that they were going to follow her home to find out where she lived. " Thank goodness you were there. That might have been something from a horrific novel if you'd not been."

She wanted to be mad at Zander, but she couldn't be when the men were helpful. Olivia was suddenly afraid of her parents if they were looking this hard for her place. If she didn't know that they were looking for her, she shuddered to think what they might have done to her had they caught her. Suddenly afraid, she locked her door and put a chair under the handle. It might not do much, but she wasn't going to take any chances.

Olivia knew that she wasn't going to sleep at all that night and blamed it on her parents. What other links would they go to in order to get to her money? She didn't want to think about that and went to bed. She'd call Zander in the morning and thank him for having her followed.

~*~

Zander was preoccupied with what had happened last night. He'd had bodyguards on her for a reason; he just didn't expect there to be an actual reason for them to be used. He was going to have to take this more seriously than before and have her move in with him. They might know where she lived at the moment, but they were working hard to find out. Something that he should have expected.

Having to go to court in the morning wasn't something that he wanted to do. But David needed to be put in jail, and the only way to do that was to bring forth the evidence that he had and put it out there. There had been some new developments since his first time before the judge. Seven more women had come forth and were saying that he'd done the same to them. He wanted the man in prison, not hanging out at the county jail, where he would be pampered.

" I have a question for you." He looked up from his work and decided that he needed to take a break once in a while. His head was killing him, and he could barely make out the person in front of him. " Are you all right? You look like you've not slept in a month or so."

" No, I'm fine. I have a headache, that's all. What can I do for you, Dusty? I'm all ears for you." Dusty sat down, but he didn't say anything for a few minutes. He finally shook his head and told him what he wanted. " I can do that for you. But since when do you need an application to buy someone's shares? That's never happened before, has it?"

" They're looking for big hitters. And with you going over the contract for me, I want you to see if that means they're looking to raise the prices of the shares on their own. I think I've already decided not to invest. This all seems sort of shady to me, but like you said, it's nothing that I've ever seen before." He took the contract and looked over the first page while his brother went on to explain why he wasn't going to invest. " I usually can take into account when some new place is selling shares, but this was a little out there. They contacted me and then sent over the contract for me to sign. They want it back by nine tomorrow morning, too. Which to me is another red flag."

" I'd not sign it. My pet peeve is having spelling mistakes in the first paragraph. They have three. Also, the date is wrong. If they want to sell you shares in the morning, then the date should be that. It's from five years ago. That could be another typo, but it also means that they're going to try and get you to owe them back-dated money." He handed the contract to his brother. " Also, and this is just me looking it over quickly, there is no mention of their name. They are calling themselves the party of the first part and nothing else. You were right to bring it here, but I think you had already decided."

" Thanks. And yes, I had, but I wanted to make sure that I didn't miss out on a great opportunity just because I didn't like the way they were going about this. It seems too quickly too for them to want money. Like in the morning? That's just too fast for me to want to invest." He stood up. " Thank you very much. How about I buy you lunch, and we call it even. I know you said you had a headache. But it's probably because you've not eaten since breakfast. It's gone past three now."

" That's it. I believe you're right." He stood up too and pulled his jacket off the coat rack. " I've been getting the new stuff ready for David Sheen and his pretrial notes. I think the judge will have a different opinion of him when I show him that seven more women have come forward about him. That's a total of about sixteen women that he's worked with and abused. One of them is still recovering from her injuries that happened just over a year ago."

" Christ. And the school didn't do a deep background check on him when he applied?" He said he didn't think that they'd done one at all. " Elaine should sue the school and him. That'll make them sit up and pay attention next time they have a new candidate to apply."

" We can only hope. I mean, you should be furious about it more than I am. You have kids who go to the school there." He said that he was waiting for the end result. Then, if he didn't like it, he was going to enroll them in private school. " That might be what I do if I ever have kids. Or find someone to marry."

They were out the door in no time and on their way to the little diner in town. Main Street Eats did a good job for lunch, and he enjoyed seeing all the pictures of the main street in different flyers around the rooms. He ordered a burger and fries, and Dusty did the same. They were having a salad too and were nearly finished with it when their meal was brought to them.

Zander had to slow himself down before he

made himself sick. He was so hungry that he was tempted to order three more burgers so that he'd make it to dinner. As soon as he ate his first burger, he made himself sit there talking to Dusty while he decided that he really didn't need a second burger. Dinner would be soon enough, and he could hold off until then.

" You really were hungry." He told him what he had been thinking. " Isn't this Wednesday? Your cook is off tonight. You might as well get yourself something to eat now, or you'll have another headache before you go to bed. And that's not good."

" You're right." He ordered a second burger plate to have the fries. That was one of his favorite foods was French fries smothered in barbecue sauce. When it was brought to him, the first plate taken away, he did feel much better and was able to actually taste the second one. " I'm going to have to set myself an alarm about eating on Wednesday. Usually, Hari will bring me something in when I'm working, and I'll eat it without thinking. I hate having a headache."

" I do too. It's something that you don't want to have around four kids." They both laughed. Dusty really did have four kids, and he'd never seen him happier. He had adopted the four kids of Shipley's family, and they had one on the way. He envied him on Christmas morning. It was going to be a madhouse and so much fun with all the little ones around. " What were you going to do for dinner tonight? The reason I'm asking is that Shipley and I were going to have a late dinner, and you can come and join us. The kids eat around six, and by the time we wrestle them to bed after baths, it's usually after eight."

" I can't. I'm sort of seeing someone." That perked his brother right up. " She's having trouble with her parents getting to her, and I'm going to see if I can convince her to stay with me so that I can keep her safe."

" Are you in love with her yet?" He told Dusty that it wasn't like that. He and she were just friends. " So was Shipley and I. And it turned out that I fell in love with her like within an hour. For some reason, it happens fast between us and our wives."

" I don't think of her like that." He thought of the one time he could see her heavy with his child, but didn't bring that up to his brother. " She's a personal shopper at the big store in the next town over. They had a fairly large mall there that she worked in. Have you ever used one of them? I'm telling you I'd recommend her to anyone. I've got all of my shopping done the day after Thanksgiving."

" All of it? Christ, we're still looking at things for the kids, and we know our delivery people by first names. Shipley wants to go all out for their first Christmas with us." He said that was what he'd been thinking. That since they were a big family now, he wanted to get everyone something. " That's awesome. You're usually the one who is still shopping on Christmas Eve. What are you going to do with yourself if you're not shopping? Come over to the house."

" I'll let you know. I do have two meetings on Christmas Eve that I have to take. I didn't set them up, but Alex did. It was the only time that she could get them all together. I'm ready for it, as you probably guessed, but it's going to be difficult getting them to pay attention with everything that is going on that day." He asked if Alex and Locke were going to be there too. " They are. They're not thrilled about meeting that day either, but like I said, it was the only time that we could get together."

After they were finished eating, they sat around and talked for a little bit. *Main Eats* closed at five, and he didn't want to make someone have to stay over just because they had time to sit around. At four, they both left, and he was dropped off at home. Glad now that he didn't drive, he was happy to go to town to see when Olivia got off. He wanted to make sure she was safe.

Since he had no idea if her parents would be there or not, he was pleased to find her Aunt Mae there. She said that she was doing a little shopping and was hoping to have dinner with her favorite couple. He didn't bother correcting her on them being a couple, but told her that it would be up to Olivia. He had no plans. He did catch a glimpse of Olivia working, and he wondered how many people would know that she didn't much care for her job. She seemed to be really good at it, and he loved watching her work.

" You're falling in love with her, aren't you, young man?" He said that he didn't think so, but he did like to hang out with her. " Yes, I can see it in your eyes. You either have a great deal of lust for her, or you love her."

" Why can't I have both?" They both laughed, and he smiled at Mae. " I just want to keep her safe from her parents. They were planning to follow her home from the hotel last night to see where she lives. I have a couple of bodyguards with her as we speak. She called me this morning to thank me for doing that. I didn't expect her to be happy about having them around."

" She's smart enough to know when she needs help and won't be afraid to ask for it either. That's something that I taught her." He thanked her. " You're so very welcome. So your plan is to stick to her like glue and make sure that Caroline and Hubert can't get to her. That sounds like something someone in love would do. Do you plan on taking her under your wing for the duration?"

" I plan on doing what it takes to keep her safe.

I don't know what they'll do to her, but it won't bode well for them to try and hurt her." She asked him again if he was in love. " No. But that doesn't mean that I won't help someone just because of that. I like her a great deal and don't want her hurt by anyone."

" You love her." He was getting annoyed by her professing that he loved her niece, but he didn't care right now. He needed to make sure that Olivia was all right and would be forever if that's how long it took him.

After she was finished with her customer, he made sure that she knew he was there to take her home. She seemed relieved, a bit fearful too, and that worried him a bit. He wondered if she'd seen her parents today, and that was why she was happy to see him. Whatever it was, he didn't like the fear on her face. He still had his guards on her, but wasn't sure where they were at the moment. Looking for them, he still kept an eye on Olivia.

" She's been working all day. And when she went to break, we went with her. Even sat with her for a time. She's been all right." He didn't know what was wrong then. " Perhaps she's a bit afraid of her aunt. She wasn't fearful until she came around. I could be wrong, but I don't think so."

" I'll talk to her and see." The older of the two men nodded, but he didn't look convinced. " What else have you seen today? Something that I should know about?"

" The one that you pointed out, her aunt? She was talking to her parents when they came by today. I don't think that the young lady saw them together, but I don't know. She's been acting like she was fearful after that, like we said." He wondered aloud if the aunt was somehow in on them, finding her all of a sudden. " I don't know, sir, but that's what I think too."

He'd have to look into things to make sure that the aunt wasn't helping her parents. The more he thought about it, the worse things got in his head. She was forever pushing him into something, too, and he didn't care for that either. Making a decision as to what to do, he was going to get to the bottom of all of this and know what was going on. Even if he had to call in a little help from his family.

Chapter 5

" That's another thing that I wanted to say to you is that I don't appreciate you hiring people to keep us out of your banking business. What right do you think you have in doing things like that? None, I can tell you. You're our daughter, and you'll do as I tell you when I tell you to do it." She'd answered the phone ten minutes ago, and her mother had never shut up once to even take a breath. Finally, she was winding down, and it looked as if she might get to say something. " What do you have to say for yourself right now, young lady? I'm not happy, and you know what happens to you when I'm not happy. I pull out my workers, and they take care of you."

" Are you finished? You've been going on about stuff for the last ten minutes, and I've not been able to defend myself." Apparently, she wasn't finished and asked her again about her goons. She didn't actually call them that, but she knew what she meant. " Trent and Sammy are really nice men. They've been doing a good job helping me stay out of your way for the last few days. You should be happy I'm not around you right now. I have a few things I'd like to talk to you about. As for my goons. I wish I'd had them all along."

" You ungrateful bitch." Olivia couldn't help it, she laughed. " What the fuck do you find so funny? I'm not happy. Have I told you that? I want you to give me all your money right now before I have to find you and beat it out of you. You know that I will, too."

" What I know is that you're pissed off because you can't get me the way you want. Has it occurred to you that it's my money and I should be able to do with it as I see fit? And let me clue you in on a little tidbit. The plan is not giving it to you. So you can either give that up or find yourself in jail. I'm not above calling my goons in to have you beaten up for trying to hurt me. I'm sick of you thinking that since you gave birth to me, you own me." Her mother sputtered around for several moments. " I'm an adult and have been making adult decisions for a long time now. And believe it or not, I don't need or want your permission to do anything I do."

" You're going to regret this. See that you don't." She told her mother that she regretted nothing and would go on saying that to her last breath. " Which might be coming sooner than you think. You ungrateful bitch. I'm going to enjoy seeing you get what's coming to you. And when you do, I'm going to laugh my ass off."

" Well, I hope you get what's coming to you as

well, mother. I'll never be as happy as I am right now to see you get your comeuppance for all the things that you and dad have done to me." Her mother said that she was going to hang up. " You do that. I'm changing my phone number as soon as I get off the phone with you."

The line went dead, and she laid her phone on the table as gently as she could. She wanted to toss it across the room and bust it, but she'd get a better deal on her new phone if she had one to trade in. She had to keep telling herself that she was safe here at Zander's home, and she liked the big house too.

" Have you figured out what she wanted with your aunt?" She told him that her mother had done most of the talking and she'd never gotten a chance to see what they were plotting. " So you think that they're plotting? I did wonder how they figured out where you were working. You said that they didn't know where you lived either."

" No. Thank you for bringing me here. There is no telling what they would have done to follow me home last night. I slept better than I have in a long time, too." He said that he'd gotten all new mattresses when he'd redone the rooms. " It was a comfortable bed, and I appreciate you allowing me to stay here. I've never been so afraid of them as I am now. Has the background check come back on Aunt Mae? I wonder if she even has any money."

" She doesn't. As far as I can tell, she's as broke as your parents, but she's not in trouble yet with the law." She asked him what he meant by *yet*. " She's behind on her taxes as well. Not as badly as your parents are, but she's behind all the same. Also, there are no houses that she owns, either. That was a lie. I doubt very much she has a will made out. I don't find anywhere where she has an attorney that she can afford to do that."

" The things that we're finding out. I can't believe that I've been so naïve in thinking that she was on my side all this time. And all along she's been in with them from the start. I guess I'm going to have to be more careful when I'm around them. I certainly don't want to be caught alone with them anymore. They're dangerous." He said that they were stupid too for threatening her so publicly. " I do wonder at times why they had me. They never wanted me, nor did they, I think anyway, love me."

" We'll get this figured out. And once we do, then we'll be able to combat them with their own words. What I mean is, we can use what they say to you against them and have them put away until their prehearing about their involvement in the money laundering deals that are supposed to be going on with them." She asked him if he thought they were involved. " Several days ago, if you'd asked me that, I would have said no. But now? I have no idea. It sounds like something that they'd do."

" I believe you're right. They've been up to no good for all of my life, and I'm just now learning that they're not the parents that I thought they were. Or they are, and I'm just figuring out how bad they really are. I'm glad you asked me to come here last night. And thank you for not telling my aunt. I think her involvement with them is more than I thought. She was just asking me where I lived when I spoke to you about not telling her. She seemed put out about it, but I'm beginning not to care what any of them wants."

" That's probably the best way to handle them. Just not be around them. But I want you to be careful when you're out. Trent and Sammy will continue to follow you around until they're in jail or your aunt goes home. I'm hoping that they all end up in jail, but I'm not prosecuting them. You can bet that I'd make sure they were behind bars." She asked him what else he'd be doing to them. " Digging deeper into their lives. This non-payment of taxes has been going on for a long time, and it's small wonder that they haven't been caught until now. I know nothing about the money laundering. I can't find anything about it on the internet or in the files at the courthouse. Did you hear about it from them or from someone else? If they are doing it, which I don't see because they're so stupid about money, then they have to be low on the process."

Last night, they'd talked about what her parents were into. Every time money laundering was brought up, neither of them could understand how they made that work for them. It didn't seem to him that either of them seemed to understand how it worked, and Zander thought that with the deal that he'd heard of in other cases, they'd have more money than they do right now. He had no doubt, either, that they'd be skimming money off the top and taking that too. For all he knew, that's what they were doing, but he just couldn't see it happening. But he didn't have privy to all their files that were being held against them.

Olivia thought about how she'd gotten here last night. It was as if she were some kind of spy and was being whisked away by a limo. As soon as she clocked out, she went out the back door to the place and slid right into a slick black limo that was waiting for her. Trent and Sammy knew where she was headed, but they stayed behind to look like they were waiting for her to come out. Zander got a good laugh at the faces of her parents waiting in the lobby for her to come out with their goons, he told her. She'd been brought to his house and set up in a bedroom that was very nice. They'd had a lovely dinner together and talked about her family until bedtime. And since she was off today, she didn't even mind that she didn't have much to wear after taking a shower.

" Your new phone will be here by noon. It was cheaper to upgrade than it was to change your number. However, I have you on my plan now, and that will give us both a discount on them." She was going to be careful who she gave her new number to. Olivia thought it was sweet that Zander didn't assume that she'd want him to have it. He'd know it anyway on the bill, but she thought he was nice for saying that. " Your old one is charging in my office. I don't know if it's rang or not, I've turned it off. But I thought if you're anything like me, you don't know the numbers of people in your phone. I certainly don't know anyone's number."

When her new phone arrived, she was quite excited. She'd not been upgrading her phone for a while now and it was exciting to get a new one that did everything that hers didn't. As she was playing around with it, she did add in numbers like her work number and Zander's, but no one else's just yet. There were thirty-six missed calls and a lot of voicemail messages. Her family rarely text messaged her, but there was one from her aunt asking her where she'd gone the previous evening. She might well not tell her either. Olivia didn't trust any of the three of them.

For the rest of the day, she transferred things from her old phone. There really wasn't much. She did move her schedule from work to the new one and updated her calendar so she'd remember her appointments. Again, there wasn't much, but she didn't want to miss an appointment simply because she got a new phone. She and Zander talked about her job a little bit, but not too much about her parents. It was her day off, and she was going to enjoy it as much as she could.

At four, his family came over to meet her and to watch a football game on the big screen television. Food was brought in, and they enjoyed snacking all evening and yelling at the game. She wasn't used to all the noise as she lived alone, but she did have a good time with his family. Especially the women of the family. They were fun and funny to be around.

" I've been trying to get my tree up for a week now. I finally gave up and had someone come in and do it for me. With four kids, it's nearly impossible to get anything done, but I wouldn't change it for the world. I love my growing family." Shipley was beginning to show her next baby. She couldn't believe that none of the four were really their children. They acted like they'd been family forever. " That's the way we want it. Dusty can work from anywhere, and I have my moments when I need to talk to an adult, but we're doing all right for only being parents for about three months now. I'm excited to see what this one I'm carrying does to the group."

" Don't let her fool you. She's brilliant at being a stay-at-home mom. She and Dusty trade off duties, and it works well for the six of them." Alex was also going to have a baby, but she wasn't showing as much as the other two. Mandy was going to have a baby as well. " You should see them when they get all dressed up. They look like the perfect little family."

They talked about how each of them met their spouses and how in love they were from the first moment. They were all surprised that she and Zander were just friends and she was living with him. After explaining about her family, they seemed to understand a little more, but they did ask her if she was in love with Zander.

" I like him a great deal. He's my hero right now. I've never known one until now, and I can't think of a better person to save me than him. I'm only staying here temporarily, just until my parents' court hearing in a week to put them in jail. I'm pressing charges against them for trying to get into my bank account, among other things that they'd been doing to me." Shipley asked her if they'd been knocking her around. " Not this time, but yes, they do when I'm out and about. Not them, but my mom has these two goons that find me and knock the shit out of me. It's been nice having my own bodyguards while out. The way my mother is threatening me, I'd probably be dead if she were able to get to me. They think that my money should be theirs. I'm saving for my own house someday."

" There are plenty around that you can get too." They talked about the housing market in their town and told her that the school system had hired new teachers. " Jobs are coming in, too. They just opened a brand new manufacturing plant that deals with sheets out near the plant. And they're hiring on with some of the temp services, too. But you have a job, don't you?"

" Right now, I'm a personal shopper. I do it every Christmas, but this will more than likely be my last one. I'm getting sick of people and how rude they can be. That's how I met Zander. He and I shopped for the entire day on Friday last week." They all looked in the direction of the men, and Zander just happened to stand up. " He did most of the list. I just pointed him in the right direction as to what he wanted on his list. He said he's never been done before Christmas Eve before."

" He's not. Not even close." He waved at her, and she waved back. " You two getting along all right? I mean, has he told you that he loves you yet?"

" We don't have that sort of relationship. We're just good friends." They all nodded. " Honestly. I don't think of him as a potential date or anything like that. We just hit it off well enough, and he's been keeping me safe from my parents and aunt. I don't know what I'd do without him sometimes."

As the women talked, she thought about how much of a good friend he'd become. She'd not wanted to like him, but she did. She supposed that he grew on her like old spores. Laughing to herself, she wondered if there would ever be something between them and decided that more than likely not. They were friends, and that's what they needed to be.

~*~

Zander was happy that his family came over. It was an enjoyable evening watching the game on the television and hanging out with them. The food helped. There was always food for everyone when they got together, and he thought that was often enough that they should just buy a restaurant and have them cook for them. Demi had told him once that there wasn't much profit in owning a restaurant, and if their family were to show up very often, they'd be out of business in no time. They certainly could put away the food.

He was glad to see that Olivia was getting along so well with all of them. She was holding one of Dusty's kids in her arms, feeding them a bottle. He would have thought they were too old for the bottle as yet, but they'd been through a great deal and might need the extra comfort for a while. He knew that he would have had he been them.

The two boys had been in the room when their father killed their mother. And when the police showed up to arrest him, he begged them to turn their backs for a while so that he could kill the boys, too. Needless to say, it didn't happen, and the boys were safe. The children were all safe now, thanks to his family, and he couldn't love them any more.

When the game was over, he and his brothers cleaned up the living room. They weren't slobs at all, but there were some water bottles that had been turned over as well as a bowl of chips. After it was all in good order, they went to the kitchen and took care of the little bit of leftovers there were. Mostly, that meant that they ate what was left, but it was taken care of all the same. When they left, it was just him and Olivia again, and he asked her how it went with the wives.

" They don't understand why we're not in love right now. It's been two weeks." She laughed, but he could tell that she was confused. " I guess the rest of them were madly in love from the moment they saw one another, and they figured that it would happen to you too."

" They really were in love from the moment that they met. Especially Alex and Locke. She was Martha's granddaughter, and in her will, she asked Locke to take care of her. He got jealous when one of us asked her out on a date a couple of days later. It was just a formal thing that we were going to, and she was just going to hang on his arm. It worked out well, I guess, with Locke telling us all we weren't to date her." He laughed. " I think that the one who had the quickest romance was August and Jack. They were in love within minutes of seeing each other."

" I don't love you. I like you a great deal, but I never thought that I'd fall in love with someone so quickly." He said he felt the same way. That they were just good friends. " We are. Very good. And someday, if that turns into love, then okay. But for now, I'm all right with just being friends."

" So am I." He didn't know why that bothered him so much, her telling him that she didn't love him, but it got him in the chest. Shaking himself, he knew better than to mess things up with the 'l' word, so he just let it go. " I was wondering if you wanted to go to your house and pick up some of your clothing? We can be there in about twenty minutes and get you packed up, and then bring you back here. There is no point in your plants dying just because your parents are trying to kill you. Do you really think that they would? Kill you, I mean?"

" I don't want to think that they would, but I've been hurt by them before, and it came close. They've never been this mad before. And I've never been this good at hiding from them. I have a feeling that it's going to build up with them until they explode or something like that. I'm worried." He said that he was doing his best to keep her safe. " Yes, and I don't know how I'm going to repay you for it either. You've gone way beyond what anyone just meeting me has done, and I can't thank you enough."

" I don't want you hurt either." He found that he was afraid for her to get hurt, and he didn't much care for that feeling. He'd never been afraid of anyone in his life, but his father, and that was so long ago now that he didn't think he could pick him out of a lineup. " Just stick with me, and we'll get you through this. Their pretrial is Monday, a week from now. Just eight more days. We'll keep on top of things until then; we should be home free."

He thought that her parents were unstable and would do just about anything to get what they wanted. They'd proven that when they went to the restaurant where Mae was staying, they'd stay out all night just to follow her home to find out where she lived. Zander didn't trust that they'd do anything to get to their daughter, and that scared him quite a bit. He liked the other woman and didn't want to see her hurt. Just as they were loading up in his car to go to her home, his cell phone rang. It was Mae.

" How did you get this number?" She said that he'd given it to her last night. " No. I don't give out my cell phone number. I only give out my house number to people that I don't know so well. Did you happen to get it from Olivia's phone when I called her?"

" What difference does it make? I have it, and I wanted to call you to report that Olivia's parents are getting desperate. And desperate people take all kinds of chances." He told her that he was keeping an eye on them. " I just don't know what happened last night. We were set to have dinner again, and she just disappeared. And now she's not answering her phone for me or her parents. I've done nothing wrong."

" Are you helping them find her?" He thought that asking straight up would get him the answers that he wanted. " They seem to know where you're staying and when Olivia is with you. Could you be helping them?"

" I don't know what you're talking about. What a thing to say to me. Why do you think that anyway? And if they know where I'm staying and that Olivia is with me, that's just the way it is. I didn't tell them. They know that Olivia spends a lot of time with me when I'm in town." She paused for a full minute, and he didn't say anything. " Is that what this is all about? Her not answering my calls? You tell her that I'm not happy with the way things are going and don't deserve to be treated this way. If they do find out where she lives, it's not going to be on me."

" They were going to follow her home the other night, and I don't think that it's a coincidence either that they knew that the two of you were having dinner in the hotel where you're staying." She huffed at him, and he had to smile. " Did you give them her phone number at her work?"

" They knew where she worked before I told them." He nearly said ah-haw but didn't. So she had been telling them information about her and helping them find her. " Besides, there aren't too many places around here that have personal shoppers. So what if they put two and two together and figured out where she's working? They know a lot about her, that's all I'm saying."

" I believe that you're helping them. And until I find out differently, I'm going to stand by that. I have Olivia somewhere safe now, and I'm going to make sure she continues to be safe, too." She asked him where he was getting his information. " My gut. And it's never steered me wrong before. Stay out of her life, and you'll be a lot safer than she is around her parents. And if you're helping them to find her, then I'll hunt you down as well."

He closed the connection and looked over at Olivia. She has a strange smile on her face, and he wasn't sure how to interpret it. Finally, asking her what she found to be funny, she shook her head and looked out the front windshield.

" You're defending me like a hero would. So are you more convinced that she's in on this or not?" He said more so, she said that she told them where you worked. " I figured it had to be her. All I did was say that I was a personal shopper to your family, and they knew who I worked for. Not many places around here can afford that, I guess. I have two jobs right now that I'm afraid to go to because of them. I don't know what to do."

" Stick with me, and I'll get you there back and forth safely. If not, then you don't have to work. I have plenty enough money for the two of us to live like hermits for the rest of our lives." She laughed. " I'm glad to hear you laughing. I was worried that your sense of humor was all gone thanks to them."

" What am I really going to do? I can't have them causing a scene at the shop where I work, and if I were to go and wait tables, they'd surely catch me. It would be just the kind of dive that they could afford. I'm afraid for the first time in a long time." He pulled her into his arms and hugged her. It was something that he'd been needing as well. " You're going to make me fall in love with you, Zander, then what will we do? Your family will be relentless in telling you they told us so."

" I can handle them. Besides, I needed a hug as

much as you did just now." He let her go, and she leaned back in the seat, staring at him. " I'm going to have to get my number changed as well if she calls me too much more. I have no use for her if she's really helping them get to you."

" I don't either. I've never really trusted her. I guess I should have gone with my gut, too. But I never put it that she was feeding them information about me at all. I just thought that they were really good at guessing. I'll have to be careful around her from now on." He asked her if she was going to see her still. " I can get information from her, too, I think. She's too easy to get things from when I want it. I've never really tried all that hard, but I will now. And since she knows that I'm avoiding her, she'll be pleased to have me call her up and want to hang around. I'll just be more careful what I tell her."

" Please do. I don't want anything to happen to you. You've come to mean a great deal to me." She kissed him on the cheek, and he smiled. " Not that I mind, but what was that for? Are you falling in love with me?"

" I think that I am. But let's not tell your family as yet. I don't think we need the pressure of them telling us that they were right just yet." He asked if she was ready to go. " I am. I want to move out of that place now that they might know where I live. I really am afraid of them. They'll kill me if they can."

" I'm going to try my best not to let that happen. I'm going to be there for you every moment of every day until we can get this figured out." She nodded, but looked so sad. " I'm not going to allow them to hurt you, Olivia. I promise you that I'm going to do everything in my power to keep them away from you."

" I know you will, and I love you for that. However, I'd never forgive myself if something happened to you. You're on their list now, and it can't be good to be there. They'll stop at nothing to get what they want, and since I have it, they're going to keep at me until I give it to them. I'm tempted just to hand over my money to get them out of my life. But I have a feeling that they'll want more and more, and I don't have it." He held her hand while he drove to her apartment. " You're making it difficult to just remain friends, Zander. What will you do when I tell you that I'm in love with you? Run for the hills? I would. I'm not exactly a good catch for someone like you."

" I don't know what that means, but I'm all right with you falling in love with me. I'm about there myself." When they pulled up in front of her apartment complex, she was ready to get out when he stopped her. " I'm in love with you, Olivia. I've never said that to anyone before, but I love you with all that I am. I hope that I can make you happy."

" You already have. And I love you as well." They got out of his car and headed to her place. He was surprised that she lived in such a crappy neighborhood, but he knew that she was saving her money for a house. He hoped that she liked the one that he had, he wanted her to be happy about their hopefully long life together.

Chapter 6

Olivia couldn't believe how many people were there for the pretrial of her parents. She knew a few of them, people who had had dealings with her family before. Up front and right next to her was her aunt. She seemed to be pinched about something—a word that she'd gotten from the kids and wondered if it had anything to do with her. Not that she cared much. She was going to tell the judge just what they'd said to her about killing her and be done with the lot of them. She'd had enough.

Zander was sitting between her and her aunt, and she loved him for that. He was her protector and hero all in one. As soon as the judge came out of his little room, everyone stood up. When he ordered them to have a seat, everyone sat but her aunt. She didn't know what she was going to say, but she had a feeling that it wasn't going to be good things about her.

" May I help you?" The judge didn't look all that thrilled about having his routine messed with, but he was polite to Aunt Mae when he told her to have a seat. " This will go my way, and not anything you have to say will have any bearing on what I'm doing.

So have a seat like the rest of the people, and we'll get this case taken care of."

" I want you to not do this to my brother and his wife. They've done nothing wrong but just got behind on their taxes. That shouldn't have any bearing on why they're being treated this way." He asked her who she was. " Mae Simpleton. Hubert Marsh is my brother."

" Well, Ms. Simpleton, we'll have to see what evidence is here for them. I'm assuming that you're not here to pay the back taxes either?" She said that she didn't have that kind of money. " And neither do they, it seems. We frown on people not keeping up with their taxes, but it's not just taxes that they're here for. There is the matter of them laundering money for the local drug dealers."

" I object to that kind of talk." Her father stood up and was told to have a seat. " I will not. I'm going to be honest with you, sir, and tell you like it is. I haven't any idea how it came about that I was laundering money. We're behind on our taxes a bit, but that doesn't mean that we are doing this other thing."

" It says here that you were taking the drug money and putting it in the bank only to take it out a month later on the pretense of having home improvements. From what I've seen here before me, there were no such improvements made on anything having to do with your house. What do you have to say about that?" He asked to have it explained to him why he couldn't put money in the bank, then take it out. " Because the money was used for drug deals and you were a part of it."

" Yeah, we did do that, but it wasn't paying us as much as it should have been, so we stopped doing that. Had I known that the money would stop coming in, too, I might have rethought that. It was nice having all that money in the bank for when we needed it." The judge told him that it was against the law. " I know that. But it was too good a payoff not to do it. But like I said, we don't do that anymore. That should count for something."

" You've just admitted to money laundering, and that's a federal offence. Not to mention not paying your taxes at all is something that goes to the state level. We need people to pay their taxes for road improvement and the like." Dad said that he didn't drive all that much and his roads were just fine. He didn't think he should have to pay for other people's roads. " Unfortunately, it doesn't work that way. You're making a good case for yourself in going to jail. Is there any other tidbit that you'd like to impart? I'm sure you've been up to no good on other things."

" My daughter has money. Make her pay our taxes so that we don't have to beat the shit out of her to get it. She's been uppity lately and deserves what's coming to her." The judge asked if he was threatening his daughter. " It's not like she helps us out at all. I mean, why won't she give us her money when we need it? We didn't raise her like that."

" I'm sure that you didn't. What kind of threats have you made against your daughter? Since you're being so honest so far, I'm hoping that you continue." Dad told him that they had threatened her with killing her, but that wasn't going to work. If she were dead, there wouldn't be any money coming in. " No, when you're dead, you don't usually have a job that you can get money from."

Dad looked confused and turned to look in her direction. She didn't know at first if he was looking at her or his sister, but as soon as he sliced his finger across his throat, she knew that it was directed right at her. The judge asked him what he was doing in his courtroom, and Dad, being honest and all, told him.

" I want her to realize that she's not going to get away with this crap anymore. She's not being a good person to us, and we don't care for it. She should want to help us. We don't beat on her all the time anymore, and I think that should go for something." The judge looked at her and asked her to stand up. " See who she's with? One of them Erickson fellas. They have all the money in the world, and we shouldn't have to beg her for money. Just get it from him."

" Are you begging her for money, or are you threatening her? That's a huge difference." Dad said that he was doing both, but she wasn't listening to his begging all that well. " I see. So you've decided that what she has belongs to you, and you're not above hurting her to get it. Is that what you're telling me?"

" Yes, you got it. She's not playing fair, is all I'm saying. She should be made to do what I tell her, and that should be the end of it. She's not very smart in the first place. Why would she be saving money in the first place if it's right there to spend? I don't understand today's generation. Buying a house isn't all that it's cracked up to be. It's expensive having a home that you have to pay taxes on and keep up with the upkeep of the sucker. All it does is drain you all the time. I'm just saving her a lot of aggravation. You see that, don't you?" The judge looked at her again and told her to have a seat; he'd get to her later. " You go on ahead and make her do what I tell her to do. It should be a law about that. That parents are the rulers of their kids until they up and die. And if she keeps this up, she's going to be dying a lot sooner rather than later."

" I think that I've heard enough." Dad finally sat down and seemed satisfied with himself. He thought that he'd won this round, but she still didn't know what to think that the judge was going to do. " Mrs. Marsh, do you agree with your husband on the things that he said today? It's very important that you be honest with me as well."

" I'd have killed her when she was born to us had I known she was going to be this much trouble. Kids are the ruination of the world, and I will stand behind that. She's nothing to me other than what I can get from her. And since she has money, then she should—Hubert didn't mention it, but I will. She blocked us from getting into her accounts. The banker was going to have us arrested for trying to get into her accounts at the bank. How stupid is that? I'm telling you right now, if you don't do what we want, this isn't going to go well for you either. I'm sick of having people hound me for money all the time. Why can't she just turn it over and be done with it?" He asked her if she'd just threatened him. " You take that anyway you want to, but you'd better be doing what's right by us, or there will be hell to pay. I'm just being honest with you, like you said."

The judge looked like he didn't know what to do. He'd just been threatened again, and she knew there were laws about that. When he asked her to stand again, she told him that she was fearful for her life. And that she'd been beaten by them before. Shaking his head, he said that he was going to give them what they deserved, and she would be safe. Giving them what they deserved could be all kinds of things, she thought with a frown.

" Mr. and Mrs. Marsh, I'm going to have you arrested. Why you've not been so far is beyond me, but it's going to happen now. You'll spend the rest of the month in jail here in town, then you'll be remanded over to the local prison until such time as your trial can be—"

" No. That's fucking not going to work for us. We'll have to be out to get her money." The judge said that she'd be safer while he was in jail. " She won't be. I'll just have my sister do what's right to her. This is fucking stupid." He was told to watch his language. " I will talk the way that I want to, and you're going to take back—I was honest with you, and you held it against us. That's not right. You should be killed where you stand. I'm not going to go easy here either. You should be murdered, and we'll be free."

" Take them away." He looked in her direction again and asked Mae what she was going to be doing. When she stood up, Olivia was worried that she was going to tell them that she'd have nothing to do with them. Instead, she told them that she'd do what was necessary to get her brother out of prison. " I thought you'd say that. So, in the interest of keeping Ms. Marsh safe as well as myself, I'm going to have you sitting in a jail cell just like your brother. Take her away, too."

She was still sitting there when her aunt pulled

out a gun. How she got it in the courtroom was something that she'd think about later. But right now, she had it pointed right at her. When Zander stood up and punched Aunt Mae in the face, it was all she could do not to run to him. But he was wrestling with getting the gun from her aunt when it went off.

Olivia didn't move. She was sure that someone had been hurt by the shot, but she didn't know who. Getting up and walking slowly to the two of them lying on the floor, she knelt down just as the police in the room started scrambling. She was knocked away from them and fell back on her ass, but she wasn't going to give up that easily. As soon as she saw the blood pooling under her aunt's body, she just knew it was going to be Zander. When the police rolled Zander off of her aunt, she feared the worst. There was blood all over his shirt, and things just blacked out.

She must have been out for a while because when she woke up, she was lying on a gurney still in the courtroom. Zander was sitting in a chair, and he looked all right but for the blood all over his shirt. She said his name, and he looked at her and smiled.

" I'm all right. I can't come to you right now because I'm covered in evidence. I so want to hold you." She started crying. " Don't love. Please? It's been hard enough just sitting here while you were out. I'm just fine. Your aunt is dead, but I'm just fine. I promise you that nothing happened to me other than I got blood all over myself."

" Is any of it yours?" He laughed that laugh that made her think she'd caught him off guard. " So long as you're safe, I am too. Why am I on this thing when I could be sitting next to you?"

" You fainted, and they were worried because you hit your head when you went down. They're going to run you in for some tests just to make sure that nothing happened. The police are taking full blame for you being hurt, too, so do what they want. They're a little on the nervous side right now." She asked if her aunt was really dead. " Yes. She was trying to kill you when I jumped up and stopped her. The gun went off when she pulled the trigger. I think she was hoping that she killed me, then was going to get you. I don't know how she got in here with her gun, but people are going to be fired for this."

" Good." He laughed again and was asked by one of the officers if he needed anything. After assuring them that he was all right, he turned back to her. " Are you really all right? I have to tell you something. When I heard that gun go off, I thought for sure that she'd killed you, and I decided that I love you very much."

" I love you as well. It just took us a bit longer to get there than it did the others. I'm all right with that. I love that we became good friends before we became husband and wife. You will marry me, won't you? I need to know that you will be my wife."

" I will. Not terribly romantic right now, but it will be a story to remember for our children. 'Dad proposed to me covered in blood while I was rushed to the hospital for possible head injuries.'" She pretended to be thinking on that. " Maybe that's why I said yes. You'll have to ask me again in a few days. I might have a head injury that is making me think that I love you enough to become your wife."

" I'll ask you every day for the next month if you'll continue to say that you love me." She said that she could handle that too. " I love you, Olivia. So very much."

" And I love you. And will for the rest of my life. Hopefully, there won't be any more people carrying guns around us for a while." He said that he'd like that as well. Then he was asked if he could change his clothing into something else. When he was given a pair of scrubs to put on, she wondered what sort of evidence he might have on him that they'd need his clothing. She realized that she didn't care so long as he was all right. She was taken to the hospital a few minutes later to have some tests done.

She didn't want to leave him but knew that he was going to be all right. She was still nervous about leaving him, but with all the police around, she wasn't too worried. He'd be just fine, she kept telling herself.

~*~

Getting to the hospital just as they were taking her down for an MRI, he sat in the room that had been hers in the emergency department and waited. He'd already talked to Locke, who was the doctor seeing that Olivia was all right, but he wanted to see her and touch her now that he was no longer being detained.

" She's going to need a few stitches in the back of her head. The officer who pushed her out of the way feels bad about it. The department is going to pick up the tab for the two of you, and I'd let them. They're still trying to figure out how Mae got into the courtroom with a loaded gun. Someone will get their asses handed to them if I don't miss my bet." He said he was just glad that he'd been there, or there was no telling what would have happened to her. " Mae will be tried for attempted murder. I know that she's dead, but that's what I heard from the officers."

" Yes, for the estate to pick up the billing for other things that will come from this. She'll also be charged with having a gun in the courtroom. Also, the fact that she threatened the judge. He will be put in protective custody until such time as the Marshes are put in prison. I have a feeling that that's where they'll end up after all this." Locke told him that he was going to keep Olivia overnight just to make sure that her head wasn't going to cause her any pain. " I'm going to be right here with her. I hope you understand that. I've fallen in love with her, and she has me as well."

" Good. It's about time." They both laughed. " I have some clothing in my car if you want it. Those can't be all that comfortable to wear when they don't fit you right. I have to wear them so I've gotten used to them, but you don't have to."

" I'd love that, but I want to wait until Olivia comes back here. I need to make sure that she's all right. I'm sure that she wants to make the same about me." Locke told him that she shouldn't be much longer; he'd go get the clothing for him. " Thanks. I owe you one. Just make sure that she's going to be all right, big brother. Now that I've found her, I find that I can't be without her."

" That's wonderful news, Zander. I wondered if she would be the one for you. We've all been hoping that you and she would be a couple. Alex really loves her already." He said that he did as well. " I can tell. All right. As soon as you get changed, I'll make sure she has a room with a recliner in it for you. They're not the best to sleep in, but it's better than a hard chair to sit up in all night."

After his brother left him, he heard from the rest of the family. They were making sure that he was really all right, and he couldn't believe how sobby he was getting because they cared enough to talk to him. As soon as Olivia was in the room with him and the nurses were finished with her, he went to the bed and kissed her.

" How's your head?" She said she was much better now that he was there with her. " Locke is getting me something else to wear, so I'll be out of these things. He also told me that he was keeping you overnight, so in the event your head hurts or something."

" They told me down in the MRI department that I'd be staying. I only wanted to see you, so I didn't pay too much attention to what they were saying." He told her what Locke had told him about Mae. " She was going to kill me. I keep thinking about that, and I'm terrified all over. She actually pulled out a gun and was going to use it on me. And would have if not for you."

" I told you that I had you." Holding her hand, he kissed her again. " Will you still marry me? I'm counting on you having to be asked a great deal."

" I'm hoping that you don't change your mind and stop asking me." He said she didn't answer him. " Yes, I'll marry you. I still have a crazy family left to get to us."

" I'm not worried about them anymore. I have a feeling that they'll be in prison before the end of the day. The judge will not take too kindly to being in the room where a gun has gone off. He'll have them put away for a good long time after what was said in there today." She held tightly to his hand and said her head was hurting. " Something that I learned from Locke is not to let the pain get ahead of you. If you need something for it, ask so that it doesn't take longer for the meds to help you."

Using the call button for her, he asked the nurse for something for pain for Olivia. While she was getting something for her head, he went into the bathroom to change. He wasn't going to tell Olivia about the powder burn he had on his belly. It didn't hurt, but he knew that it was going to be tender for a few days. Also, he had the beginnings of a bruise where he'd fought Mae for the gun. He was alive, and that's what he kept telling himself.

While she dozed off, he sat watching her. A couple of times his phone rang, but since it wasn't his family, he didn't answer. Whatever anyone had to say to him, if they left a message, he'd call them back. Otherwise, he was going to spend this time getting to know Olivia.

He thought about how he'd wrestled a gun from a mad woman, and his heart would skip a few beats. He'd done it to save Olivia and would do it again if necessary. He hoped never to have to do that again, but he was willing for her. For any of his family. As the darkness of the room made him sleepy, he laid his head on her hand and closed his eyes. He knew that it was stress that was making him tired, but being with Olivia really helped.

Waking up when someone came into the room, he was told that they had to take her blood pressure and to wake her because of the head wound. He made his way to the bathroom again and, while washing his hands, realized how hungry he was. He'd not had anything since breakfast, and it was nearly ten at night. While in the darkness of the bathroom, he called Dusty. He knew that he'd be up this late and asked him if he'd mind bringing him something to eat.

" I was just thinking about you. What do you want? I can pick up anything you want or bring you leftovers. Never mind, you don't want that. We had chicken nuggets and French fries. I don't even think there was anything left anyway." He told him what he wanted. " I can pick that up for you. By the way, it's all over town that you saved Olivia in the courtroom. People are calling you a hero."

" I just did what I needed to do to make sure that she was all right. I promised her that I'd take care of her. To be honest with you, it wasn't until the gun went off that I realized what I'd done. I told myself I'd do it again, but I can't believe I did that the first time." Dusty told him he'd rather he didn't do something like that again. " You'd do the same for Jack, and we both know it. However, she would have taken the gun from her before shots were fired and knocked her on her ass. She's good at shit like that."

He made his way back into the room and found the lights on. He asked Olivia if she was hungry too, and she said that she was. Dusty said he'd bring them both in something to eat so they'd not starve to death and would be in soon. He sat down next to the bed when he got off the phone.

" I've been thinking about what you said about my parents going to prison. Do you think they'll really go there? It would be nice not to have them in the same town as us. I mean, I know that I should feel bad about them going away, but all I can think about is how they said that they never wanted me in the first place. That hurts." He said that it would him too. " Tell me about your parents. They can't be as bad as mine, can they?"

" Worse. Our mother left us with our drunk, abusive father when I was barely five years old. She couldn't take it anymore. On top of that, she said that she wasn't going to have any contact with us, and for us not contact her either. We didn't. She was selfish for leaving us behind, and I'll never forgive her for that." She asked about his dad. " He was a drunk and would beat us daily until we got bigger than him. Since he was drunk all the time, it took him a week to figure out that we'd left home. He would get mad at us for the stupidest reasons and beat us for it. We got to the point where we didn't have all that much to do with him. Locke never spoke to him again after he said he'd been cheating on a school test in his senior year of high school. Then we won the lottery."

" Really? Is that where all your money comes from?" He told her that in addition to them winning the biggest lottery to date, they'd also inherited a great deal from Martha Grable. " I've heard of her. She owned a big house on Main Street up until she passed away."

" Locke inherited that from her and a lot of her things. That's where he and Alex are living. We all did get something from her estate." She said that was wonderful. " I miss her every day. She'd be so happy to know that we've all found wives and are living the way she taught us to. She's the reason that I became an attorney. And that Dusty is a financial wizard. We all owe our lives that we have now to her. But I'd give it all back to have one more day with her. She was that special."

He told her how they'd left home one afternoon by getting into a van at a friend's house that Locke was at to play chess. He told her how they'd been so terrified that their father would come after them that for three days on the way from Ohio to where they live now, they didn't dare tell anyone who they were.

" Then we pulled up in front of Martha's home when our van finally died. She invited us into her home, and after cleaning up a bit, she invited us to stay with her to keep her son from knocking her around and stealing her money." She said that there was a lot of that going around. " No kidding. I never realized that until just now. How can people profess to love someone that they plan on knocking around a great deal? I'll never understand people for as long as I live."

" I can see that too. I see the worst of people, too, I think. Working in retail, people think that you're not human or something. They treat us like we're nothing but there to cater to them." He nodded and kissed the back of her hand. " You're the best thing that has happened to me. I hope you know that."

When Dusty arrived with their meals he didn't stay long. He said that he had diapers to change as it was his turn. He wondered if he'd ever be happy about changing diapers and thought that it was all on his brother. No one could be that happy and have to change crappy diapers.

After they ate, she only ate about half of her sub. He watched as the nurse gave her something more for pain. She said that it hurt badly now that she was away from all the things going on and just wanted to rest. He didn't blame her; that's all he wanted to do, too. Getting into the recliner, he thought for sure that he was going to end up on the floor and was careful how he got in and out of it. All he needed to do was to break his fool head while staying with Olivia while she recovered.

Chapter 7

Being released from the hospital, she was happy to be going to Zander's home. It was a great place to live, and she really enjoyed how he had it decorated. Not to mention, the house was warm and cozy all the time, especially when it was snowing outside like it was now. Careful walking into his home, she was happy when he said they could have lunch ready in just a few minutes. Stress was making her hungry, and she wanted more than just a salad to eat.

Olivia was glad to be home. Her head still hurt, but not as badly as it did the first few days after it happened. The police had come by and made sure she was all right a couple of times, and she was fine with that. It was them that had caused her to get hurt in the first place. However, she wasn't going to hold a grudge against them simply because she'd been injured. She might well need them soon, and didn't want them to not come because she'd been a terrible person.

" I've been thinking about a few things." She asked him if it had anything to do with her parents. " Yes and no. Mostly to do with our living arrangements. You should give up your apartment and move in here permanently. Also, you might not have been told this, but your parents are going to be spending the next year and a half in prison for threatening the judge. They won't be able to get out on any kind of loophole either. They're there for good until their trial."

" That's the best news that I've heard in a while. Thank you for telling me." He said it was his pleasure and told her that he loved her. " I love you as well. I'm so glad that you needed to get your shopping done before the end of the season. I've never had so much fun as I did that day."

" I had fun too. You made it easy for me to get what I wanted." He took her hand into his and kissed the back of it. " I can have us married in the morning if you want. No pressure, but since you're saying yes to my popping the question, I'm going to hold you to that."

" I'd love to be your wife. But I want you to know that if you get tired of me soon, I'm going to be very disappointed in you. My heart will be broken as well." He said that he'd never do that to her. " I'm happy to be your wife. I love all the things that come with being her, too. Like this house. I couldn't have afforded anything like this, and I love it."

" So you're just marrying me for my house? I see how you are." They both laughed, and she was happy to know that he still found her funny when she was dealing with things that were upfront in her mind. If he did get tired of her, she didn't know what she'd do. " I do love you, Olivia. With all that I am."

" And I love you as well, Zander. I can't wait until things settle down for us and we can live a good life with each other. It will be great knowing that we have each other until we're pushing up daisies." She hoped that she had that long with him and decided that she wasn't going to be looking for failure when they were doing so well together. " Now, what about sleeping arrangements? I know that we've never talked about sex, but I'd love to have you in my bed with me as soon as possible. I don't even care if we have sex right away. Just knowing that you're beside me will do me a world of good."

" I'd love to have you in my bed. I've thought of nothing else but having you beneath me while I make love to you." She felt her body respond to his words, and she felt her heart skip a few beats. " I want to taste you when you come in my mouth. I can't wait until we get to that point in our relationship so that we can become one together."

" Oh my." She had to shift in her seat in order to make herself more comfortable. He was making her needy, and they'd not even touched each other as yet. " Are you ready for bed? Or wherever you want to make love? Right now, I could come with just you kissing me. You do that so well, too."

" I love you." He pulled her into his arms, and she had to adjust herself over his lap. Once she was sitting straddling him, she felt his erection against her pussy. She could feel herself weeping for him, and she wasn't sure what to do about it. As soon as he pulled her blouse off, she knew that they were going to make love right here in the living room with nothing to stop them.

He made love to her breasts. Suckling at her nipples, they were painfully full, and she knew that she was close to coming. When he stood her up and laid her against the couch, he removed her pants and panties in one move. Once she was naked, he stared at her like he was taking inventory of her body. Touching her hands to her breasts, to give them some relief, she was thrilled when he growled low in his throat. It made her come in a short, hard punch to her body.

" I'm going to feast on you. And when I've had enough, if that's even possible, I'm going to make love to you until neither of us can stand up. Are you all right with that?" She grinned and told him that she was more than all right with whatever he wanted to do to her. " Good. I'm going to enjoy this."

Turning her so that she was sitting up with her legs hanging over the couch, he spread her legs open, and she was embarrassed at how wet she could feel herself getting. As he lowered his head to her, she held her breath. Sure that he would make her come quickly, and didn't know if she wanted to come so fast. As soon as he blew his hot breath over her pussy, she came hard, crying out with his name on her lips.

When he suckled on her clit, she came again, knowing that she was going to be coming a lot more until he was finished with her. As soon as he slid his fingers into her pussy, tightly and slowly, she came again. Her body felt buzzed for some reason, like it was waiting for the most epic climax she'd ever had. She'd had so many so far that she was sure that there was nothing left that she could give. Lifting his head up, she told him that she needed him, but he said he wasn't finished. Pulling him from her pussy again, she begged him to fuck her so that she could come. Grinning at her, he moved up her body and stood before her.

" I'm hard as stone and am willing to bet that as soon as I enter you, I'm going to come. I'm going to jerk off all over you so that I can make it last." Her body heated up by his words, and she nodded, unable to speak beyond the lump in her throat. " Will you help me come? I want to feel your mouth over my cock."

Reaching for his belt, she pulled it off with his help. Once he had his pants undone, she couldn't wait for him to pull them off. She needed him so badly that she took him into her mouth and ran her tongue over his crown. He was thick and long and wondered if he'd fit inside of her. Just as she was enjoying herself with him in her mouth, he pulled away and came all over her face.

Christ, it was like he'd been saving up his cum just for her. As he fisted himself, she knew that she needed to come again and touched her fingers to her pussy. Touching herself, she came crying out his name again. Her entire body hummed with the release, and she didn't think she'd be able to move for a while before he pulled her up from the couch and bent her over the back of it.

His cock filled her almost as soon as she was in front of him. As he fucked her hard, she held onto her breasts and pinched her nipples. When he leaned over her and kissed her shoulder, she nearly came apart with just that. When he said that he was coming, she held on tightly to the back of the couch and screamed when his first bit of cum filled her. He fucked her harder than she'd ever been fucked before, and she couldn't seem to get enough of it.

Leaning over her, he didn't move. His cock was still hard inside of her, but she was exhausted. When he finally moved, pulling her atop him when he sat down on the couch with him, she decided that she was going to do this every day just for the feelings that she was having. Making love to Zander was liken to putting your finger in a light socket, it was that good.

Moving off him, he groaned and seemed to hurt when she sat on the couch next to him. She could barely move and was happy that they'd made love. Sore now that things were settling around her, she laid down on the couch with him atop her. Once he was happy with the way he was lying, she closed her eyes, telling herself that she just needed a nap for a few minutes and nothing more.

Waking up, she was in their bedroom. Zander was on his phone beside her, and she sat up to look at him. Smiling at her, she felt the weight of the world lift off her shoulders and a new, wonderful kind of weight pulling her more in love with him. She asked him how they'd gotten up here.

" I sort of half carried and half dragged you up here. You seemed to want to sleep more than you wanted to wake up for me." She asked him if he was all right. " I'm spectacular. How about you?"

" I feel like I've made love to the man of my dreams and I'm a little sore from it." He told her that he had a hot tub right outside the room if she wanted to get into it. " I need a shower first. I feel sweaty."

They showered together, making love again against the tile. She could feel herself falling more in love with him with each time he touched her, and she loved him so much already. Once they were in the hot tub together, they enjoyed just talking about their day. Olivia had never been this in love with anyone, and she doubted that she'd ever love like this again. If he decided to leave her now, she'd never survive it. It would just kill her to lose him after being so in love with him.

After getting out of the hot tub, they went to bed. They said that they only needed to rest up a little bit before finding them something to eat. She was hungry and decided that if she went to sleep now, she'd never wake until morning. Her body was so relaxed that she knew that on some level, she wasn't going to be getting up anytime soon. They made their way to the kitchen to find something to eat.

" She usually puts out sandwiches when I skip dinner. Here we go." He pulled out a platter of roast beef sandwiches and ham ones. " I love Hari. She's the best cook of all the cooks in the family. I'm going to miss her when she retires. There won't be another person like her to come and take care of us."

" There was another woman in here the other day when I came into the kitchen. She said she was teaching her how to make sausage gravy and biscuits for you. I was told that was one of your favorite meals. It's mine too, with a little bit of cheese on the top." She ate two of the sandwiches and some of the potato salad that was in small containers in the fridge. " I haven't had any of that in a long time. I'd forgotten how good it was on a cold morning."

" I love to have it right before a big trial. It calms me down for some reason." He moved to sit beside her, and she smiled at him. " I can't seem to get enough of you. You're all I ever thought about when I was thinking that there might be a woman out there for me."

" I never thought that I'd find my one true love in you. It's why I kept pushing you away. Fat lot of good it did me. You worked your way into my heart anyway. And I couldn't be happier." He said he felt the same way about her. " I don't know how I survived without you all my life. Now it's almost as if you've been there for me forever. I can't wait to see what the next fifty years or so brings up. Do you want to have children? I'd love to have more than one. I was an only child, and I hated it. However, maybe I was lucky in that. They might well have turned out to be just like my parents."

" I'd love to have children with you. However many you want." She said that she thought that two would be enough. " I'm willing to keep practicing with you until you're ready."

" I might be broken if we keep making love like we did tonight." He said that he loved her and couldn't wait to have children with her. Then he told her about the first time he'd met her and how he'd seen her in his mind, heavy with their child. " That's so sweet. And we didn't even love each other then. I do love you, Zander, and will for the rest of my life."

" We'll be married in the morning, then we'll have to plan for a honeymoon. Someplace warm. But we'll have to wait until after Christmas. It's in a couple of weeks now, and I can't wait. Everyone is going to have wives for our first Christmas together, and Martha would have been so proud of us all."

Getting back into bed, they were snuggled up against one another before falling asleep. She couldn't get enough of Zander holding her, and he seemed to have the same feelings. Closing her eyes, sated and full, she knew that she was going to have the best day of her life tomorrow and become Mrs. Olivia Erickson. She couldn't wait.

~*~

It was three days before Christmas, and he was getting excited about having his family come over to his house on Christmas Eve. They were going to be hitting all the homes of each other and exchanging gifts. Then on Christmas day, they were going to meet at his house for dinner and fun. He had the biggest house by far and was willing to host his family every year if asked. He was happy to be able to have them come over for all the holidays.

Zander was glad that he and Olivia had gotten married yesterday. They had planned for it to be the day before, but they didn't get up until after noon and were too late for the planned wedding. All his brothers stood up for him, and their wives stood up for Olivia. It was about as big as a home wedding would have been with the dozen or so of them there. He couldn't have been happier with the turnout. Even the weather cooperated in that the sun was shining and the snow was piled high off the streets.

" There's some speculation about the Marsh family and them being put in different prisons. A source told me that they're plotting when they're together, and it doesn't bode well for the other inmates." Zander asked Demi what he meant by that. " I have a friend who works the kitchen out at the prison. He said that he'd heard that since they were in the same prison together, they're making trouble for others around them. And when they do get together, not as often as they'd like, they have their heads together like they're planning a big cue or something. He said that the officers are trying to keep them apart, but it's difficult to do with so many prisons there."

" That's just what we need. Them having people on the outside doing their bidding. Do you suppose they will be separated? I mean, I couldn't believe that they were put in the same prison in the first place. Hell, I didn't know they had coed prisons, and I'm an attorney." Demi told him why they were coed. " I guess I can see overcrowding as an issue. I never really gave it much thought. But I can see them getting into trouble with their plans. They just don't think that the law pertains to them in any way. Have you heard anything about how they're going to do that? I mean, separate them?"

" He told me that they usually move them in the middle of the night. Just wake them up and tell them that they're going someplace and take them there. It works out better when the people are about half asleep. Plus, there isn't any trouble with the other inmates when it's done that way." Zander nodded and looked at the plate of food in front of him. " You didn't care for it, did you?"

" No, I love it. I just wish I'd have known that I was going to be tasting for you today. I wouldn't have eaten so much lunch before coming here. I really love the chicken salad. The grapes in it are perfect. And are those raisins in it?" He told him they were cranberries. " They're perfect when you take a bite and bite into one of them. I love the sweetness of them, too."

" I forgot to put walnuts in it. But I suppose that's all right with you since you can't stand them." He said that he thought he might like them in the salad if he were to put a few of them in it. " I will next time."

They talked about the other items on the list of food he was trying out and decided that his brother was an excellent cook. He asked him about cooking for the school still, and Demi said that he was having fun with that.

" The boys eat on the days that I make pancakes. Usually they eat at home, but on those days. I'm having a lot of fun seeing all the kids, too. Even some of the parents are coming in to have some breakfast and helping to clean up afterwards. It's been working out well for the system, and I get to spend more time with my kids." Demi had two little boys with Mandy. They were her nephews, and they'd adopted them. His brother was great at being a dad, and he was going to come to him for advice when his own kids came along. " I'm sure going to have fun when our own children are going to school there. I might be doing this until I'm in my eighties and still having fun."

" I can see you doing that too." He told him he didn't care for the pie he'd made, and Demi was all right with that. It was too sweet, and Zander had a sweet tooth, too. " If I think it's too sweet, then you know that it's sweet."

They talked about the prison moving the Marshes around and other topics that came to their head. That was why he liked hanging out with Demi.

He was the one brother who could keep up with his conversations when he was jumping around. When he was ready to leave, hating that he didn't have more time to spend with his older brother, he got a much-needed hug. When asked why he needed it, he told him that with the holidays coming up, he seemed to miss Martha more.

" I know what you mean. That first Christmas with her was a blast. Even Thanksgiving, too. We'd never celebrated those when we lived at home, and it was nice to be able to spend our first one with her." Demi agreed. " They only got better as the years went by. This will be our first Christmas without her, and I find myself wishing that we'd had one more year with her."

" I wonder if that would have been enough with her. I mean, we'd say that we only wanted one more with her, then there would be the next with her because of all the kids we're going to be having." He said he'd not thought of that. " I think about her a great deal. Without her, there is no telling what we'd be doing with our lives. I know that we'd not be as wealthy and happy as we are right now. She taught us that."

" She taught us a lot of things that I still use to this day." Demi agreed. " I just wish the women could have met her. I know she would have loved them all as much as she did us." He decided to change the subject.

" They're calling for snow tomorrow and Christmas week. I hope it's not too bad that we won't be able to travel. I know that most of us have four-wheeled drive cars, but if it gets too deep, we might have to postpone getting together until it mellows out."

" I'm going to each of our houses even if I have to walk. I want this holiday to be epic, and there will be no snow deep enough to keep me from doing that." They both laughed and knew that they'd have to postpone the holiday if it got too bad. But since it rarely snowed all that much where they lived, they thought that they'd be all right. " The kids are so excited to be having Christmas this year. I think it's their first one where they're going to get gifts. I know how that feels for them."

" I know too. It's been a long time in coming, and I'm looking forward to having my first holiday at home. Who would have thought that we'd be having wives this time? Not to mention children on the way and here too." Demi said that he was going to make the holidays special for his kids every year. It's been a long time in coming around for them, and I want them to have something to look forward to all year. They all believe in Santa Claus still, so that makes it fun too."

After they parted ways, Zander made his way home. Olivia was working today at the store, and he was happy for her. She seemed to be enjoying her work more simply because she didn't have to worry about her parents anymore. He knew that it did him good knowing that they couldn't come to get him.

Getting home in time for dinner, he decided that they were going to have his favorite meal. Once the biscuits were made up, Hari baked him a couple so that he'd make it to dinner time. With a bit of honey on them, he really did enjoy them while waiting for Olivia to get home.

" I'm home." She came in the door and was covered in snow. " It's really coming down out there. I hope that it only goes for a bit longer. I don't want to be snowed in this week. It's the busiest days of the store, and I'm really booked up."

" I would imagine that you are. Those people who wait until the last minute are nuts." They both laughed because he'd been one of those last-minute shoppers until this year. " How have the tips been? I'm betting good."

" Not so much. People are just angry about the prices and having to pay me, too. I got to the point today that I just wanted to tell them all to fuck off and to leave me alone. I didn't have any robe shoppers today, but it was just as bad. Who buys their wife a vacuum for Christmas and thinks that she's going to be all right with that? That's something that you might buy for the house because yours broke down, but not as a holiday gift." He said that he'd keep that in mind if they needed to get a sweeper. " You'd better. I'd hate to have to hurt you over one. Get this, this guy bought one of our top-of-the-line sweepers that also doubles as a carpet cleaner. He bought all the attachments, thinking that she'd love it even more. I would have vacuumed his dick right off of him had he done that to me."

He loved it when she got all riled up like she was. She had no filter when she was angry about something like gifts. He really was going to remember that for the future and tell his brothers about it, too. There wasn't any point in them being in trouble with their wives when he could save them the trouble.

Tomorrow she had to work again, and he was tempted to tell her to stay home instead. She seemed kind of depressed about the gifts that people were buying for their spouses. He wondered if the wives were telling him to go to a special shopper, hoping for something romantic, at the very least something that they wanted rather than something that they could use around the house. A lot of wives were going to be disappointed when they opened their gifts in the next few days.

He'd been shopping all day for something for Olivia. He had given her a plain band for their wedding and was hunting for the perfect diamond to go with it.

As soon as he saw the one that Martha had left him, he knew it would be perfect for her. After having it cleaned up again, ready for her finger, he decided that it was going to be wonderful to give it to her. He hoped that she loved it as much as he loved her. It was thoughtful and not a robe or vacuum cleaner.

After dinner, which was a huge hit, they settled in the living room to watch the snow coming down. Around seven o'clock, it began to taper off, and he was glad for it. Just knowing that she was going to have to be out in it tomorrow made him nervous. He was going to get her a new car too for Christmas, so he'd not have to worry about her getting stuck in the snow that they had. He might just give it to her today so that he'd not have to worry so much. It was in the garage along with a giant bow. He couldn't wait for her to see it.

Another thing that he'd gotten her was some lingerie. Mostly, he figured that he'd bought it for himself, but he was excited to see her wearing it. She was so beautiful that every time he saw her naked, he couldn't believe that she was all his. If he could paint, he'd love to do her in the nude so that he could hang it in their bedroom. It was his dream to have her looking loved whenever he wanted.

" We need to get ourselves a television for the family room. I love watching the fireplace in there when we're in there together. And with the weather being like it is, we would be warm if the power were to go off, I think." He said that he'd only lost his power once since living here, and it had been a godsend to have the gas fireplace back there. " Then it's settled. We'll get ourselves a larger television for back there after Christmas. There might be sales we can hit up to get one cheaper. What do you think?"

" I'll say it again, you're brilliant. I love the way that your mind works, too." She snuggled up to him as the news was on, and he noticed that she'd fallen asleep. Holding her until they were ready for bed, he knew for the rest of his life he'd be as happy as he was right now. He just couldn't tell her enough times how much he loved her and still feel good about it. She was his heart's desire and his only true love.

Chapter 8

Eight years later

Locke watched the kids playing outside. It had been a long winter for them, being couped up in the house, and he was glad that they'd been able to come outside today. It surely did his heart some good to know that they had an outlet for their unbelievable energy. He looked over at Alex, large with their third child, when she said his name.

" We are going to regret this child, I think. As full of energy as she is now, I can't imagine what she's going to be like when she's their age." He just smiled at her, knowing that they'd love her as much as they did her sisters. " I can't believe that we're going to have three little girls in the house. I thought for sure this one was going to be a boy. All your brothers had boys. I wonder what happened to us?"

" I'm thrilled to have little girls around. They certainly do know how to keep their uncles in line. And they're aunts too, for that matter." His phone went off, and he knew it was going to be work. He was on call today and wasn't looking forward to going in. "

I have to go in. I'm sorry, love. But we knew this might happen."

He was retiring from being a doctor. This was his last weekend to be on call, and he was disappointed that he'd have to go in once more. Getting up from the lounger, he made his way into the house to get changed. He'd take a shower too, so that he'd be ready when he got there, and was happy when his daughters were disappointed that he had to go in too. They were the light of his life.

Driving into work, he was stopped at the light when he realized that he had forgotten to pick up his cell phone. Oh well. Anyone needing to get in touch with him would call home, and Alex would help them with whatever was going on. As soon as he pulled into his parking place, he was inside before he could change his mind and go home to get it. He knew his home phone number and that of Alex's, so if he needed something, he knew that she'd be there for him. As soon as he walked into the room of the patient he was there to see, he knew something was up.

" Mrs. Randle. I thought that you had another month to go. How are you feeling?" He checked her out and was happy to see that she wasn't in labor. " I wonder why they called me in today if you're not about to deliver."

" I've been having contractions all day and last

night too. I thought it was those pre-contractions like I had with my other one, but this one is getting me in the back something terrible. I think Roland is afraid I'm going to deliver at home like we did the first one, and he's not taking any chances. He did all right, but he's been a nervous wreck since I found out that I was going to have another baby." Back labor wasn't uncommon, and he was willing to make sure that she was in good hands.

" How about if I put you on the monitor and we check them out. If it's nothing, you have nothing to worry about. If it is labor, we're going to have to slow you down because it is still too early for you to give birth." He had the staff hook her up to the monitors. They didn't show much, but he could tell that she was uncomfortable. " How about I give you something to relax you for now? Then we'll keep an eye on you for the rest of the evening."

" I'd like that. If for no other reason than Roland is all right. He is freaking out at home with our other child, and I don't want him to drive if I don't have to have the baby just yet." Locke agreed with her, telling her that having a baby at home isn't the ideal situation. " No. He doesn't want to deliver our next child. He's made that perfectly clear. On several occasions."

After giving her a little bit to relax her body, he was glad to see that she was resting. It took a lot out of a woman to give birth, and with one at home himself, he knew some of what she was going through.

Hanging around his office, he got some much-needed paperwork finished up and ready to hand off to the next doctor who would take his place. He'd met the woman and was glad that she was the kind of doctor that he would have picked himself, but he just wanted to be home and not have to work anymore. He loved spending time with his family. All of them.

It helped that he had a seemingly endless supply of money. He'd never told anyone but his wife that he had won the lottery twice more, and one of them was a big Powerball payoff. He'd told himself after the second win that if he ever won again, he would retire, and when the big ticket had all his numbers on it, he decided that it was time for him to do what he'd promised her. Alex was thrilled to be having him home all the time, and he couldn't wait to spend more time with his children while they were still young.

He'd shared with his brothers, of course. That's the way that he did things. And when they won, never as much as their first time winning, he knew that they shared with him. Even when they won scratch-offs, they shared with him, and he thought it was funny. He never needed the money, but it was nice to have it all the same.

He never wanted to be as broke as he was when

he'd been living at home with his brothers and father. That was hard times. He still found himself to this day worrying about money coming in. But Alex has taken care of them with her way of thinking outside the box and finding new ways to save money. She was his hero.

By three o'clock, he was ready to go home. Just as he was getting on the elevator to go out the door, Alex and his two daughters came off. They were all dressed up, and he couldn't help but be proud of them. Asking them where they were headed, he picked up Martha and kissed her on the cheek.

All his brothers had one child named after Martha Grables. Either a first name or a middle name, each of them had named their child after the woman who had taken care of them when they first moved to Tennessee. She was their true hero in their lives in saving them from not being just men, but men of worth who had made something of themselves.

" You forgot your cell phone, and since we know that you'd need it, we decided to come by and see if you could have a late lunch with us. Then we could all go for ice cream." He said he thought that was a great idea. " Sarah has it in her head that she wants to eat where Daddy works. I hope you don't mind, but I told her that would be fine. That way you don't have to leave if you can't."

" I was just leaving, but we can eat here. I don't

want to disappoint my favorite little girl." He picked up Sarah and was holding them both when the elevator opened for them to get back on. " I have a patient here, but she's going to be going home soon. Then I'm free for the rest of the day."

Just as he got onto the elevator to go down to the cafeteria, he saw his brother, Dusty. Wondering what he was doing here, he nearly called out his name. But the doors shut, and he thought that he had imagined it, so he didn't bother with telling Alex. She would think he was crazy, and he didn't need her teasing him today.

Once the doors opened to the cafeteria, he got off telling Alex about his day so far. He didn't think anything about it, getting off on the floor that he'd been on a million times before, but there was music playing, and he'd never heard that before. He eyed Alex hard.

" What have you done?" She told him she'd done nothing. He looked into the vast room that was the dining area. There were hundreds of people there, and they all looked like they were there for him. " I told you I didn't want any kind of party to commemorate me leaving."

" I had nothing to do with it, only to get you down here when I arrived. I was so worried that I was going to miss you. You just had to forget your phone today, didn't you? Anyway, we were to get you down here so that they could celebrate you." He walked into the room only to be greeted by *Congratulations* and *happy retirement* from the group of well-wishers. " This is all on the other women. I told them what you wanted, but they weren't going to hear it. So act like you're having a good time, or so help me, I'm going to brain you."

It was going to be hard not to have a good time. There was a cake with his name on it and happy retirement. Also, balloons that his daughters enjoyed. People came around to talk to him, asking him what his plans were now. Even his brothers were there with their wives and families, and he couldn't have been happier.

He saw Beth Randle there with her family and went up to speak to her. She was the reason that he'd come into the hospital today. Asking her how she was doing, she told him that she really was having contractions, but it worked out that she'd been able to get him there. He hugged both her and her husband, thanking them for the great start to his party.

For the next several hours, he was subject to a lot of jokes and well-wishes. There was not only staff there that he'd worked with over the past fifteen years, but patients that he'd seen too. A lot of them showed up and left early, but he was glad to see them all. As soon as he got to his sisters-in-law, he told them how grateful he was for them getting this organized, but not to do it again. He didn't much care to be the center of attention under any circumstances, and this was right up there.

" We love you and can't stand the fact that other people can't show you how much they love you, too." He told Shipley that he was going to have her a belated party. " Too late for that, I'm afraid. Besides, I never really retired. I just take less dangerous jobs now that I'm out of the action."

He was also glad to see Carrie there. She had a baby in her arms, and he thought that it suited her. She and her new husband had been adopting children, as she couldn't have any children of her own. It made his heart feel good to see her so happy after all these years. She was the best family friend that any of them had ever had.

When he finally found Dusty, he asked him what he'd been doing on the upper floors. He looked embarrassed, and Locke thought that was funny. He told him he'd been looking for him.

" Alex said you'd forgotten your phone, and I was worried that you'd leave without coming down here. So I was going to go find you and have a piece of pie with you. But I saw that Alex and the girls had found you, and I had to sneak out of the third floor and head back down here. I'm surprised that you only saw me the one time. I'd been wandering around this hospital for an hour before you made it down here for this thing." He asked him how he kept track of where he was at any given time. " I got lost between elevators."

" I've been here every day for all this time. You sort of have to find yourself landmarks." He hugged his brother. " Thanks for helping out. I think that Alex and the girls kept the secret really well."

" The one I was worried about was little Brandon. He had it in his head that it was your birthday, and we had to keep telling him that it wasn't. That's why when he saw you, he kept saying happy birthday to you." He said he had wondered about that. " Kids are wonderfully helpful when you want them not to tell someone something. Aren't they?"

He picked up one of the gifts on the gift table and opened it. He was just curious what sort of gifts someone got for a retirement. It was a book on pooping in the bathroom, now that he had more time. He was still laughing about a couple of the reasons one would give to take more time in the bathroom when August found him.

" How are you going to do this with all the extra free time? I don't know what I'd be doing if I didn't have a job to go to every day." He said he'd figure out something to do with his spare time. " With Alex ready to go at any moment, you can't go too far. Why don't you guys take up camping? It looks like something that the five of you can do."

He was the only one who hadn't taken up camping when the others had. It wasn't that he didn't care for it, but there were other things that he loved to do more, like spending the night in a hotel with a nice mattress and pillows. Laughing, he told August that, and they both laughed at how pampered he wanted to be when he was 'camping'. He'd gone on trips with them, but he stayed in an air-conditioned room rather than out, where they had to learn a whole new thing just to be able to sleep at night.

" It's not for us." August told him he didn't give it a try. " And I don't see myself giving it one either. I love my comforts, and since I can afford them, I'm going to use them. Sorry, but no thanks. Besides, it's too much like working when I'm on vacation, and I don't want to do that. As I said, it's not for us."

August walked away laughing and telling anyone that he walked by what a party pooper he was. He didn't care. Camping wasn't for everyone, and he'd be the first to say it wasn't him. The thought of driving someplace in the middle of nowhere and setting up camp didn't appeal to him. He wanted someone to come in and make his bed and clean up after him. He didn't want to have to worry if his dirty water tank was going to have to be emptied before he was ready to leave.

~*~

Dusty picked up his oldest son and put him on his shoulder. He was cranky and tired, and if he got a short nap, he knew he'd be better. Besides, he loved holding Markus when he was all soft and ready to sleep. His energy levels could be through the roof sometimes, and it was nice to be able to hold him still for about an hour. He looked over at his lovely wife and smiled.

" What?" He said that he loved her. " You're not getting lucky tonight, buster. I've been with the president all day, and I'm ready to curl up and take my own nap. How did he ever get elected with him being so stupid about shit?"

" I'm sure you know the answer to that." She'd gotten him elected when his numbers were way down. All she's done is tell him where the air strike had to land, and he was reelected nearly overnight. " You have any idea how much I love you, Shipley? You're the best thing that has happened to me."

" I love you too, you big nerd." Ever since they'd been married, she thought him to be a nerd. Just because he loved numbers and how to make them work for him, he thought of himself as a financial wizard. Shipley thought of him as a nerd. " Markus will need to have his bedtime changed if he sleeps much longer than an hour. I'm not staying up all night with him. I'm really exhausted."

" I got him. It's my turn to be up anyway." They'd always taken turns with duties that had to do with their children. He will never forget the time Shipley was to entertain the Vice President of the United States, and it was her turn to do diaper duty. She did it right there on the chair that was next to her while talking to him. It was a sight to remember, and he would always love her for being the best mom there ever was. All his brothers took turns taking care of their children, and it seemed to suit them all.

" Markus looks comfortable. I wish I could join him." He grinned at his brother, Locke, and told him that he was going to be taking a lot of naps from now on. " Not so much. As soon as our baby comes this time, I'm going to be a stay-at-home dad. I'm looking forward to that. Alex is still working for the foundation, and I don't think she's going to be quitting anytime too soon. She thrives on that job."

" She gets to talk to adults all day is what she loves. You'll soon be begging one of us to come over and talk manly to you. You're going to be knee deep in tea parties and dress up." He said he'd enjoy it too. " I'm sure you will. I know that I missed that part with having three sons. Are you guys going to have any more?"

" No, this is it for us. How about you?" He said they were going to try one more time for a daughter, then that was it. " You know the old saying? How if you have more than one sex of a child twice, the rest of them will be the same."

" I'll take my chances." Moving Markus to his lap while he slept, he looked at Locke. " I can't believe that all of us named one of our children after Martha. Markus was as close as I could get after Demi had a boy named Martin."

" I'll let you in on a secret. Martha hates her name. I tried telling her that she was named after someone great, but she won't have it. The kids at school tell her that she's an old woman. I wish I had thought of that when she was born, and I would have made it her middle name. She's getting teased a great deal." He asked if her uncle had to step in and take care of her. " I don't think so yet. But I'll let you know. She thinks of you and Zander as her favorite uncles. And only because she has the two of you wrapped around her little finger."

" That she does. And when she's all grown up and dating—yes, I think it will happen, I'm going to be the uncle that double dates with her until I know the boy as well as I do her. And he'll have to deal with Shipley, too. She's overly protective of your girls as well." He didn't laugh with Locke because he was serious about his duty as the favorite uncle. " All three of them are going to have a hard time dating as far as I'm concerned."

The party was winding down when Markus woke up. He didn't seem to be in that good of a mood until Locke took him into his arms. For an eight-year-old, he loved to be cuddled. He thought that was all on Shipley and him being their firstborn. The two of them could cuddle up and be asleep before he even got the movie started on movie and popcorn night. He wouldn't trade that for the world.

He had three sons and loved each of them. Shawn, the middle one, was the thinker in the family, and he didn't get into as much trouble as the last one did. Dusty didn't know if it was because he was thinking up the plots or thinking of ways to get out of them, but he was rarely, if ever, in trouble, not like Markus and Kevin. They were ready for anything at any time so that they could be in the middle of all the action that was going on.

When his son went off to play with his cousins, he leaned back in his chair and watched the people in the room. Locke was doing a good job of mingling around the room, talking to people, but he could tell that he'd rather be anywhere but here. He wasn't the type of person to be up front in front of a crowd.

He'd never forget the first time he realized

how special Locke was as a brother. He'd given up everything so that he could be a nurse for Martha when she got into her golden years. They'd all had jobs and homes, but he'd stayed with her until the very end. Making sure that she could have her one request granted and die at home. He'd done that and more for her while the rest of them had gone on with their lives like nothing was in their way.

It wasn't as if they didn't love her. They all had and thought of her as the mother figure they'd never had. But when she'd gotten ill that last year, it had been Locke who had stayed with her night and day to make sure that she wasn't in any pain when she took her last breath. He'd done that for her, and he'd never regretted it once.

When Shipley said that she was ready to go, he gathered up the boys and made his way to his brothers. He would tell them all goodbye, as if he'd never see them again, when they were to have dinner together tomorrow night. The six of them would meet weekly on Thursday night just to be together. The wives did the same thing on the same night, too.

On his way home, they stopped for dinner. While there had been cake and vegetables around, there weren't enough calories in it for three growing boys. Their favorite place to eat was fast food; it didn't matter what kind, and that's where they went. He could enjoy a good burger, too, but his favorite was pizza. He could have that every day and all day if it came from the place on Main Street. Shipley said that she didn't care for it and that had gotten her booed by the four of them. She was only kidding to get them going, but it was fun.

After dinner of burgers and shakes, they went home. Summer was just making itself known to the area, and he was looking forward to it. He and the boys would enjoy the pool year-round if it were heated, but theirs wasn't, so they had to enjoy it when they could. Most of the warmer months they'd be found outside around the big pool, and that was true of the other homes too. All of them that didn't have pools had put one in so that they could have the comforts of jumping in when they were hot and having a good splash.

That night, when the boys were getting ready for bed, he marveled at how big they were getting. Taller than some of their cousins, he wondered if they'd take after him. He was just over six feet five inches and towered over most of the other brothers. The only one that was taller than him was Zander, and he was six foot seven inches tall.

After getting the boys to bed and reading them a story, he went back to his office to finish up what he'd been working on when they'd had to leave for the party at the hospital. It was the quarterly reports for each of their investments and how much they'd made or lost. There were a few of the latter of their spreadsheets, and he was happy for that. Printing out the sheets of paper, he knew that he'd give them to them tomorrow night, but they'd not look at them until they got home. That was their time with family, and he knew no business was discussed while they were together. It was a good rule that he actually loved and was glad that they all abided by it.

Going up to bed around midnight, Shipley was already asleep. She really had worked hard today, and he didn't blame her at all for being asleep before he got to bed. Crawling in beside her, she wrapped her warm body around his and snuggled up under his chin. He was nearly asleep when she spoke to him.

" I've been thinking about what we're going to do this summer with the kids. I'd love to take them to DC and let them see the places that we've been to before without them." He asked her if that was a good idea; they were terribly rambunctious. " I know, but I'm in the mood to see all the sights again. We haven't done that since our honeymoon. If they get too much out of hand, we'll drop them off at my sister's house and go see the sights without them. You know that she'd be able to handle them without any trouble."

" Yes, but she's married to the president now, and she might have a bit to do on her calendar." They both giggled. Amanda had married Brad Hayden when he'd been vice president, and they were the happiest couple that he'd ever known, with the exception of them. " She really does have a lot on her calendar. But I know if we were to ask, she'd clear her schedule and take them for the day. Can you imagine what the Oval Office would look like with their four and our three? I shudder to think what the people in the offices might think of us if we were to do that."

" I was just kidding. She would take them, however. Even if they had to go to some party that she and Brad are headed to. I love her to pieces, but there are times when I think there's something wrong with her. Who likes to be around that many kids all the time?" He said that she'd always loved children. " Yes. And with her expecting another one, it's hard to believe that she's going to be the mother of five soon, and living in the White House. They wanted a family man in the office, and they certainly got that when he was voted in."

" Yes, I'll say they did." He continued to hold Shipley while she laid in his arms. At some point, she must have fallen asleep again and he watched her. She was the most beautiful creature that he'd ever seen, and he didn't tell her often enough, he thought. As she rolled away from him, getting to her side like she liked to sleep, he thought of the first time he saw her and was blown away once again that she was his.

When he woke up the next morning, he was alone in the big bed. He could hear the kids down the hallway and wondered what they could be up to so early in the morning. Getting up to get a shower, he knew that he had a few things to finish up before tonight, so he wanted to get a good start on them. As soon as he made his way to the kitchen, he realized it was much later than he'd thought. It was nearly lunchtime for the boys.

" I'm making grilled cheese for the boys, sir. What would you like to eat with them?" He told their cook, Andrew, that he was all right with grilled cheese, too. And soup. " Tomato is what is simmering on the stove if you'd like that. Or I can get you some veggie soup that was left over from the day before yesterday."

" Tomato." Nodding once, Andrew said he'd get right on that and asked where Shipley was. " I thought she'd be right here in this mess, as I know she loves grilled cheese sandwiches."

" She had to take a call. It couldn't be avoided." It was from the president then, and he nodded. " The boys are set to head to their aunt Mandy's home today. She has some project for them so that they can work for her. Then there is the party for their oldest's birthday. Mr. Demi is picking them up so that they can be there on time. He said that you tend to be a little late when you're busy."

" Good. I don't have to leave until I'm ready." Shipley joined them in the kitchen then and had herself two grilled cheeses and a bowl of soup. She said that she was expecting some papers today and would he mind if they came in through his fax machine. " Forgot your number again, did you?"

Laughing, she said that she had, but it didn't matter. His was as secure as hers was, and that was all that mattered. As soon as the boys were picked up and he was in his office, Shipley joined him. After getting her paperwork, she was off to her own office to do what she did best. Keep America safe from the bad guys.

Chapter 9

August was going over his second book when Jack joined him. He still couldn't believe that she was his after all this time. Every once in a while, she'd put on a red dress, and they'd have fun. The two of them still owned Erickson Landscaping, and he couldn't have been happier.

" Are you about finished with your book? I just heard from your publicist that it was going to come out in the fall." He said that he was just going over some of his notes on it and was just about ready to send it off to the editor. " Good. We'll have to celebrate tomorrow night that you finished a book. I love giving you a goal to look forward to when you work so hard."

He didn't have to ask her what she had in mind. It wasn't as sexy as one would think, but just the two of them going out to dinner. Someplace with cloth napkins and a place where they could be waited on. Not too many restrictions, but they still had a good time even when they got home that night.

" It's been a long time since we've had a real vacation. How about we plan one with the boys and then have some fun with them. I heard that Dusty and

Shipley are going to DC again this year, and that might be fun too. I know that the kids would enjoy it." He said that it sounded really fun. " Don't just say that because you think that's what I want to hear. I really would like to go to DC with them and see the sights. I've never been there before. I want to see it all."

" I wasn't kidding. I think that would be fun. Maybe we can talk the others into going as well and make a family vacation of it. Maybe even Locke would be up for that. You know how he loves to go camping." They both laughed at that, and she sat down in the chair across from his desk. " Something else is on your mind. What is it?"

" I was just thinking that the anniversary of my brother's family deaths is coming up. It depresses me to think that he thought that the only way out was to kill his family and then himself. I can't imagine wanting to take the lives of my children over facing the reality of life. I wish I would have known what he was going through. I would have tried to get him some help." August told her that he hid it well right up until the very end. " I know. That's what depresses me so much this time of year. It's been eight years now. His sons would have been teenagers." He just watched her as she cried.

" I love you, Mandy. So very much." She came around to his side of the desk and sat on his lap. He loved holding her like this, and when she yawned for the third time, he found himself falling asleep by just dozing off. " If you lay here much longer, we're both going to be sore from waking up in an odd position. Why don't we go to the living room and lie down?"

" I'd love that, but I have work to do. There is going to be an auction of one of the smaller landscaping firms next month, and I want to look up some prices on what things might go for. I don't know that I want any of their equipment, but it might be nice to get a few things. So long as they go cheap enough." She stood up, and he watched her. " Thanks for letting me vent to you. I know that I'm being a sad sack, but sometimes it just hits me that they're gone. No one should have been able to take the lives of children. I just get depressed about it sometimes."

" I understand. I do too. If you ever want to vent again, you know that I'm here for you. I love you." She kissed him on the mouth and moved toward the door. " When I see the others tonight, I'll bring up about heading to DC. They can talk to their wives, or you can bring it up when you meet with them. Whatever happens, it will be a good time for us with the kids."

Just as he was getting to work again, his cell phone rang. It was Zander, and he wanted to tell him that he was going to be running late tonight. He had some paperwork to file, and the courtroom was busy.

He told him that he'd be all right with that and asked if he'd spoken to the others.

" I have. You were the last one on my list. I should have called you first, as I know you'll be early, but I wanted to let the others know what was going on. Did you hear that there was a big to-do at the courthouse today? Something about renovations going on, and they found some old records that had been boxed up for about fifty years. I would love to go over some of them sometime, but they're going to have to have them gone over by the Feds because of where they were found. I wonder what someone was thinking by hiding them away like that." August said that he'd not heard, but he'd been in his office all morning. " I'll let you know what I can find out. It might be something that you can write about one day when they're released. Wouldn't it be awesome to be able to know what sort of judges they had back then? I would love to be asked to help with them. It might be an eye-opener to see what judges were doing back then."

" You're thinking about them being corrupt, aren't you?" He said it was what he lived for. " I can see you going over them with a fine-tooth comb and making up stories as you went over them. I can see you writing a book about them, too." He said that he'd leave that to him. " I just finished my book and was getting it ready to send to the editors. I need a break from writing for a while. Perhaps I'll be ready to start again when they release them to the public. I might just see what I can get into with them."

" Sounds great."

After hanging up with his brother, telling him that they'd wait for him at the restaurant, he nearly forgot that they were having dinner at his all-time favorite place. Their steaks were great, and he loved their blooming onions. He could eat an entire one of them by himself. He might be a little sick afterwards, but he'd enjoy it while eating it.

Getting ready for dinner, Jack had already left by then, and he decided that he was going to talk them into the trip. It would be fun to get together as a family. It had been a while since they'd done anything like that, and he wanted to spend as much time with them as he could. You never knew what tomorrow was going to bring, and he wanted to have as many memories as he could with his family as he could get.

Smiling to himself, he wondered why he was getting to be sounding so gloom and doom and decided to change things around. He had a great family, and they'd be around for a good long time. As soon as he was out the door, he realized something else. How lucky they'd been in their lives since leaving home, and he couldn't wait until they got together tonight. It was fun to be with his brothers, and he was glad that they did it every week like clockwork.

He rolled down his window and enjoyed the breeze coming in through it. Once he was at the restaurant, he was excited to see his brothers. As soon as he was in the place they reserved for themselves, he hugged them all and told them how much he loved them. They were a little shocked but told him that they loved him as well. It was going to be a great dinner, and he couldn't wait for it to begin.

Since they all had families, they didn't drink at these things. He was glad about that. He liked a beer with his steak dinner and didn't miss it at all when they were all together. As soon as Zander joined them, he hugged him too and told him how much he loved it. Zander hugged him tightly back and told him that he needed that. Just as they were being seated, his cell phone rang, and it wasn't a number that he knew, so he let it go to voicemail. They didn't leave a message, which he was happy about.

As soon as they ordered, their salads were brought to them. He really enjoyed the house dressing and was surprised when it was different. Not putting up a fuss about it, he ate his salad with the rest of them just before their dinners were brought to them. Trading around bites of food with each other, something that they always did, he got to taste Demi's chicken dish along with Dusty's mushroom sauce over his steak. It was all good, and he was happy that he'd gotten the pasta dish with his steak, as it was one of his favorite things on the menu.

" I was just talking to August about the find that they found in the walls of the courthouse. It's supposed to be from fifty years ago." They speculated on that for a while as they ate, and just like him, they wanted to read over the reports that had been found to see what things were like back then. " I'm going to see if I can get with the attorneys who are going to be a part of the files just to see if I can get a first-hand look at things. There is no telling what sort of stuff they find in those files. I wonder if some of the people from around here will be in them? I know that we won't, as we've not been here that long, but I'd love to see if anyone has skeletons in the boxes."

" I wonder how they got into that area in the first place. Makes me think of foul play. I have no idea why, but that's the first thing that popped into my head." The rest of the table agreed with him on that speculation. " It could be nothing more than just some old paperwork about the renovations that were going on at that time, but it's fun to think about."

They talked about their week they'd had too. When he brought up that he'd finished his book, the others were happy for him. August had written another book so far, and since he was loving it so much, he decided that he could make a career out of it. Not that he needed to work, but sometimes it was good to have something to do that filled out your days. And his days at times needed filling out.

After dinner, they sat around and talked about what had been going on in their lives. Mostly, it was the same thing. They loved being fathers, and they had been working hard. As they were settling back in their seats, he watched them all talking. It was something that he liked doing and was happy that he could see them at their best. It was Zander that he enjoyed watching the most. He was quiet today, and he wondered what was going on with him. Asking him about it, he said that he'd been thinking about retiring as well for a while anyway, and didn't know how to bring it up to the family.

" You just tell them. They'll understand." He nodded as if he knew that and said how he'd been working nonstop since he'd gotten out of college. " I think that we all have done that, and it's beginning to show on us. I'm just happy that I can do something different once in a while to stave off the boredom. Writing gives me an outlet that I didn't know that I needed until I started doing it."

" I don't want to write, I'll leave that up to you, but I do want to do something that takes me out of my head. As I said, I've been working nonstop since college, and while I enjoy my job, I'm feeling the pinch of being bored with it too. Like I've seen it all and done it all. While I know that's not even possible, my head and heart tell me that I've had enough. I just want to be able to sleep late and not have to worry about who is calling me for something. I don't think I've even had a day off in years. I'm forever on call for the family, and I need to be getting out of the office more."

" Tell them like that. I'm positive they'll understand. Hell, they've all about quit their jobs. Demi only does the school thing now, and he seems to be happy. I know that Locke just retired, and that's good for him. We're all getting burnt out on what we do and need a break. Look at Knox. He's decided that he wants to get into the courtroom more and has taken on some cases for the family so that you don't have to do it all." He asked him if he was trying to convince him to do it. " Now is as good a time as ever, I think. We're all together. I mean, you've talked to Olivia about it, right?"

" She's been trying to get me to step down for a month now. She misses me." He laughed. " I don't know how she misses me. I work from home most days, and when I'm at the office, it's only for a couple of hours. It's more than likely she misses me just being there for her and the kids. That's another thing that I'm missing.

My kids growing up." He said that he'd be better off retiring while they were still young. That way, he can go to plays and stuff while they're in school. " I think you're right. I'm going to do it. Starting next week. I have to finish the things that I have started for all of us. I might just make sure that I have time off in the meantime. Like an entire day without anyone needing me. That would be good to start off with, don't you think?"

" I think you should make a clean break of it and just stop. No one is going to blame you for it. As you've said several times now, you've been working since you got out of college, and it's time for you to lay some of the work aside so that you can have a good life." He nodded and put out his hand. Shaking it, he was glad that he could be there for him when he needed someone to bounce ideas off of. " Tell them now before dessert comes, or you won't get the chance. They'll want to get back to their homes soon after that. I know that I do."

Once he made the announcement, the room was silent. He looked around at his family, wondering what they'd been thinking when Locke stood up and congratulated him. The others did the same thing. While hugging him, telling him that they'd all take up the slack of needing him all the time, Zander looked relieved. Like a huge burden had been lifted from his shoulders and put away for good.

After ordering their dessert, they sat around talking about what Zander was doing, and he could tell that the rest of them were wondering why they were working so hard, too. He wanted to tell them that none of them had to work, not really, and that they all should take some time off. It was the perfect time to bring up the vacation to DC for the summer, and it went over as well as he thought it would. They were thrilled to have something to look forward to in the coming months, and so was he.

As they were leaving the restaurant, he saw that there was about five hundred dollars in tips around the table. Locke usually picked up the bill, and he was glad to be able to help the waitstaff out by making it worth their while in taking care of them for the evening. They weren't demanding by any means, but they certainly could take up a lot of time from the staff that usually took care of them.

He was glad to be home that night and was happy that Jack had also had a good time. He told her about Zander, and she said that they'd talked to Olivia about it too. She really did miss him when he was working so much, and this was going to be good for their family.

~*~

Demi was thinking about what his brother had said

at dinner about retiring, and he thought that he was ready for a change, too. His boys no longer went to the grade school; both of them were in middle school now, but his other two sons were there. He didn't want to slight them the time to spend with him, too, so he decided that until they were out of elementary school, he'd continue doing the breakfast.

That would be another six years of making breakfast for the kids at the school, and he thought that he could handle it. It wasn't like it was that hard on him to get up and get it going. He had enough help now that he barely had to do much more than supervise. Still, it was fun seeing his children as they went from their home to the school where he worked.

" I've been thinking of you working." He told Mandy that he'd been doing the same thing. " I was wondering about that. With the others quitting their jobs, it might be a good time for me to quit too. I've been thinking about it for a while now, and the classes are getting smaller all the time. Most of the classes are now only one or two people, and that's kind of boring for me. I love teaching them how to use the computer, but I think that with you home in the afternoons now all the time, I'd like to be here with you. It's something to think about."

" I'm not saying that you shouldn't quit, but couldn't they make the classes larger by waiting until they had more in the class to take them? I mean, that might be a solution." She told him why that wouldn't work. " Okay, I can see that. People want to learn quickly so that they can get a job in the market better. I never thought of the demand of you working all the time. You would be welcome here with me while the kids are in school." He wiggled his brows at her, and they both laughed.

" But seriously, I've had enough. I've been doing it for nearly ten years, and I need to either teach something else or stop altogether. I think there are enough people working there who can do the classes without me around. I just want a break like the others are doing." He asked if the women were thinking about retiring as well. " I think that pretty much all of them have decided that it's the way to go. Even if it's only a temporary thing, it would be nice to have a break. I know that I could use one."

" Then you should do it. Neither one of us has to work. It might be nice to have some time during the day to hang out with each other. I know there are times when I miss you." She said that she missed him a great deal. " Then you really should do it. Just tell Alex that you want to take a break from it all, and I'm sure that she'll understand. I know that Shipley has been voted in as medical examiner again, so she'll have a term for four years, but it happens so seldom around here that someone needs a post mortem that she could only go in a few days a month to keep up with things going on."

" Elanie said that she was thinking of no longer being a nurse. She's been at it longer than the rest of us have been, and she said that she wants to be home with her family, too. I don't blame her. She and Knox have the youngest kids, and that can't be easy, leaving them for work every day. And she has to work a twelve-hour shift on top of the post-mortem job. Like you said, that's not an everyday thing, but with working full-time as a nurse, it must be hard on her. Her baby is only two, and I don't know what I'd do if I weren't around to see the milestones of our kids when they were that little."

Knowing that she was right, he did wonder what they were all going to do with their lives if they weren't working all the time. Become lazy rich people? He didn't see that happening for very long. In fact, he was thinking that if he didn't have his books to write, he'd be bored out of his mind about now. He was always at his happiest when he was working and didn't think that his family was going to be any different. They'd been working since before coming here, and he didn't know how they'd do it without a job every day.

But he kept his mouth shut. He wasn't going to comment on anything just yet. They might well really be ready for this mass retirement, and he was barking up the wrong tree. Time would tell, he supposed, and he was looking forward to what new thing was going to bring his family together again.

Demi was going to make dinner tonight as it was their cook's night off. They were going to have homemade corn dogs and French fries. One of his favorite things to make for his family. As he began prepping for dinner, Mandy came in to help him. She didn't do much, but she was good to have around as company. He asked her what her plan was now that she'd decided to retire, too.

" I'm going to join the school PTA. Not to be in charge but to be a part of the kids' activities. It's been nice being able to have first-hand information from you when you're there listening, but I want to be a part of it for a while. At least until the boys are out of elementary school. I might like it enough to run it someday." She laughed, and he joined her. She wouldn't run it. He had a feeling that she'd only go to a couple of meetings and decide that it wasn't for her. He didn't like gossip anymore than Mandy did, and that's basically what it all was. " You said that they're having a meeting soon. I'll go just to see what's going on. I don't have to join anything to be around, do I?"

" No. Most of the people there are only there for the cookies and juice afterwards. I know a couple of people who are loud about things, but that's not for me. I only go because I'm required to by the school board, because I work there. I don't think I'm going to enjoy it as much as you might. They do gossip a great deal." She said that she didn't want to be a part of that. " I knew you wouldn't. Sometimes, it's all I can do to get through the mornings with so much going around."

" Yes, I wouldn't care for that. I'll just sit in the back and watch what goes on." He nodded as he made the first batch of fries. " I'll call the kids down. I know that they had homework, and I hope they got it done. Otherwise, we're going to be up for a while."

The rest of the evening, after dinner, they did work on homework. It wasn't as bad as he thought it would be. Just some reading to do and some math homework. It would be the end of the terms soon, and they'd have to get them into some activities around the town to keep them busy, but he knew that they'd love that. Now that their pool was in, they would spend a great deal of time sitting around it and enjoying the summer months. He knew that he was going to.

Getting them ready for bed that night, he forgot that tomorrow was Friday. He had to make pancakes for the older two tomorrow and then cook them at school for his other two sons. It was fun having the first meal of the day with them. He never tried to change things up with them anymore. Just went with the flow of things like normal. Messing with routines could cause a meltdown, and he wasn't ready for that early in the morning.

After the boys were all in bed, he and Mandy sat in the living room and watched some television. There wasn't really anything that he watched, but it was nice to catch up on the news. There was a lot going on in the news of late.

Going to bed with Mandy was always a thrill for him. She would come to bed all warm and snuggly, and he'd be asleep in no time. Once in a while, they'd talk about their day, but not often. They were busy parents of four boys, and they didn't have time to be there for them if they were exhausted all the time. He loved his growing family and was glad that he got to share it with Mandy, the one and true love of his life. Rolling to his side, taking Mandy with him, he closed his eyes. It was then that he realized that he'd forgotten to order for the school and would have to do that first thing in the morning. Glad for this time to be relaxed, he decided that when they took the trip to DC this summer, he was going to hotel it. Or stay with Dusty and Shipley in their house. Camping was fun, but he wanted to see the sights more than he wanted to be worrying about water levels in his tanks.

He was up and showered before his alarm went

off. As soon as he sat down at his computer to order the next week's food, he realized that he had done it. He was getting forgetful in his old age and decided to tell Mandy about it. She'd get a kick out of what he'd done and laugh with him. Or at him. He found that either way, he was going to be happy. As soon as he got breakfast finished up for the two who were in middle school, it was time to go to work. Demi enjoyed his job of cooking for the kids and thought he would for as long as it took to get his other two onto the next level.

After work, he decided that he needed to get a few things for home. The cook would usually order what he needed, but she was on vacation and wouldn't be back for another few days. He was enjoying cooking for his family on the nights that she was off, but he didn't want to do it all the time. The clean-up was messy, and he wanted to spend time with the kids. They usually helped him with cooking, but they usually made a mess bigger than if he did it by himself, but he never complained when they wanted to help. Spending time with them was the best part of his day.

They were going to have burgers on the grill tonight, and then they were going to make their own sundaes for dessert. It was really messy to make, but they all appreciated that time of the meal, and he couldn't turn them down when that was what they wanted. He was just leaving the store when he heard from Mandy.

" They said they'd been wondering when I was going to make the move to join you at home." He said that it was great and loved her. " I love you too. I'm so excited. I only have a few more classes to teach before they start bundling them all together. Just like you said. It'll be tough getting used to being home all the time, but I think that I can handle it."

" I'm sure that you will be able to. I can't wait until we get into a good schedule with the kids so that we can be around them more." She told him that was what she was looking forward to as well. " Good. I wonder who will be next to leave their job. It might be Knox. I know that he was hoping to have more to do with the business, but with Zander retiring, he might well do it as well."

" Let's hope we don't all go crazy with being at home all the time. I don't want us to fight all the time when we're together." He said he didn't see that happening. " I'm going to let you go so that you can finish up what you're doing."

He was home in another ten minutes and decided that he was going to make brownies to go with the sundaes. He was even going to make some hot fudge to go with them.

Chapter 10

He looked around the courtroom and decided then and there that he'd had enough, too. Laughing to himself, Knox decided that if he didn't win this suit against the family, he was going to quit anyway. There was enough evidence to win in their favor, and he thought that for as much work as he'd put into this case, he should be able to do what he wanted. He called Elaine before he started and told her what he was planning on doing.

" Thank goodness. I thought I was going to have to beat you into submission. Are you really going to retire too? I think that it would be great to have us both at home all the time. I miss the kids." He said that he did as well and wanted to see things like his kids' first games, too. " I have missed so many of them that I want to cry at night. I've decided to give my notice at the hospital today. What do you think?"

" I think that's a fan-tabulous idea." She said she was going to do it then. " Good. I'm going to tell Locke in the morning. We have a breakfast meeting to go over some contracts. I'll still do that for the family, but I'm not going to be researching everything to the point of spending weeks on a case that doesn't require it. And I'm finished with the courtroom. I thought that I'd like it, but I don't care for it. People are bastards, and I'm sick of dealing with them."

" Good for you." She laughed and said that she was going to do it as soon as she got off the phone with him. " I need to just make a clean break of it. And giving them two weeks' notice will be about the same amount of time that I have left in vacation time. It'll be nice to be home for the summer months, too."

" Yes, we'll have to find us some places to go camping this summer. I know that we both love it. And it's about time to introduce the boys to it as well." She said that Kian was a bit small yet, but she thought that he'd enjoy going on a trip with mommy and daddy. " All we need to do is load up some food and clothing, and we can be out the door. I love that about having our camper ready to go all the time."

They'd been taking quick trips since the snow melted off, just overnight places that they could get a jump on camping season. So far this year alone, they'd had five trips, and they had enjoyed every one of them. But they wanted something more than a couple of days; they wanted a month to go someplace and hang their hats.

When the courtroom was adjourned for lunch, he went across the street and got himself a hot chicken sandwich with fries and a shake. Usually, he sat in the courtroom and went over his notes again and again just to make sure that he didn't miss anything. But today he made himself slow down and experience his food. Even going so far as to just sit under the tree and feel the sun coming down on his face before going back to the courtroom. When it was time, he walked to his seat and waited before getting his paperwork out. This kind of thing wasn't him at all, and he found himself taking pleasure in the break from scrambling around like he was late for everything.

After winning his case, he cleaned up his area and spent a few minutes with his clients. They were just other lawyers from the foundation, but he rarely spent any time with anyone outside the family, and he loved that he could make the time. He felt that he was missing a great deal by not spending time with others. He'd worked with these men and women for years and didn't know anything about them.

Thinking that was sad, he wondered at the other things that he'd missed working so hard. Like his brothers, he'd been working all his life. Not even becoming a billionaire had changed him in his working habits. He got up every day with one thing in mind, and that was to work to the best of his ability and not stop until all the work was finished. Even when he had his mini vacations with his family, he could be found with paperwork in hand and his nose buried deep in records so that he had all the information needed. More information than he needed in reality.

Going home, he put his briefcase on the table with his keys and went into the living room. No one was home yet, so he pulled the remote toward him and turned on the television. Finding a movie that he'd not seen, he watched it until Mandy and the boys came home. He even dozed off for a few minutes too. It was the best two hours that he'd ever spent in a while, and he loved it.

" What did you watch?" He told Mandy what the name of the movie was supposed to be. " I don't think that got very good reviews. Why did you watch the whole thing?"

" Because I could. And I didn't answer the phone once while I was doing it. You know what? I'm going to do it again, too, when I have the chance. I can't remember the last time I watched an entire movie without having to leave it to answer a question or two. It was quite entertaining." He asked her how her afternoon went. She told him that she'd given her notice. " That's great. Did they try to talk you into staying? I would have. You're the best nurse they have there."

" They asked me to give a month's notice so that they could find a replacement. I almost said yes, but I didn't. I don't want to spend another month working when you're home. How did your case go?" He told her about his lunch and how much fun he'd had at it. " It's the little things, isn't it? I mean, we've been missing out on the little things for some time now. I'm excited about this next part of our lives."

After dinner, where the two of them had a pleasant meal, they went to the living room with the boys and played a game. He'd like to say that he finished the game without interruptions, but the boys made it so that they had to take a break to get snacks. It was the most pleasant evening he'd spent with his family in a long time. And his kids noticed that he wasn't in his office all the time, too. That was very telling for him.

Going up to bed after spending an hour in his office writing up his resignation, he felt better than he had in some time. He'd heard from Zander twice about how his retirement was accepted and was hoping that he was doing the same. All his brothers were thinking of spending more time with their families, and he thought that was the best way to go. He'd see how he felt in a month. Things might go back to the way they were, he told Mandy.

" I don't think so. I'm going to keep you so busy that you're not going to miss work at all. I have a list of things that need to be done around the house, too, that we've been putting off." He asked her what sort of things. " The rooms all need to be painted, and while I know we're going to end up hiring someone to do that, the stuff will need to be taken off the walls to be ready for them. I want to redo the kitchen too. It's really out of date since we moved in. Not a full renovation, mind you, but we do need to bring it up to this century."

They talked about what other things he was going to do. Not that he was going to be doing manual labor, he just wasn't built for that anymore, but there were lots of things around the yard that needed to be supervised as well. Like they wanted to put up a nice swing set for the kids. Trim back the trees that had gotten out of hand since the last snowstorm.

After turning in his resignation, he made his way up to bed. He so loved this time of the evening when the house was quiet, and everyone was sleeping. Going to the window that looked out over the back yard, he could see where things had gotten out of hand there, too; tree branches had fallen and hadn't been picked up by the yard crew. He wondered for a brief moment if he could get them gathered up and put into a large pile to burn. Then he realized that he really wasn't in that sort of shape anymore.

He still ran every morning with his brothers. He and one or more of them would get together and run in the morning before having breakfast. It was like when they got to go to dinner on Thursday evening together. Just a way to catch up on things and each other. It was how they were notified that he was going to have a baby in the house soon. That had been three years ago, and now they were trying for number three.

Watching the deer in his backyard, he wondered where all the time had gone and sat down on the window seat to think. They'd won the lottery almost twenty years ago now and had turned that money into a working, successful business that they all still got more money from daily. Without the help of Dusty and August, knowing the market as well as they did, he did wonder where they'd be without them. Probably still wealthy, as they still pinched pennies everywhere they could when they could.

Going to bed, he was happy that he and Elaine still had a good relationship. They didn't argue at all, and when they did have a disagreement, it was usually over before bedtime. He never wanted to go to bed angry with her, and she said the same about him. They loved one another, and he couldn't believe how lucky he'd been in finding her when he did.

Getting up the next morning, he had several voicemails that he ignored for having breakfast with his kids. They weren't accustomed to having any meal with him, so it was a real treat for all of them to be able to sit down and have a good time eating. He'd forgotten how messy they could be and was glad that he'd not worn his suit yet. Then he realized that he didn't care if it had gotten dirty or not. He had more than enough of them to last him one day. He got a phone call from Demi just as the kids were off to preschool.

" I was wondering what your day is like? I have the morning free today as it's a professional day for the students, and I thought we could hang out together. Unless you have to go to work." He told him that he did have to go in for a few minutes to see if he was able to retire, but other than that, his day was free. " Great. We'll have lunch at Main Street and then hang out at my house. I have a few projects that I need to get done, and I want your opinion on them. Nothing major. Just a few things that I've been putting off until I had more time."

" Elaine has a list of things that she wants me to supervise as well. It's a long list, and I find that I'm looking forward to doing it." He asked if they could combine their lists and get it all done by the same people. " I have to get the yard cleaned up first and foremost. It's a mess after the last storm. Then I want to start on the kitchen. It's not been upgraded since we moved in, and it's well past time."

" Kitchen work is on my list as well. I've not looked at the yard, but I'm sure that, like yours, it's in need of an overhaul as well. I know that the rose bushes out front have become overgrown and out of control." They talked about what they were going to do, and he found that he was having fun. On some level, he knew that it wouldn't last; he'd have to find himself something to do so that he'd not be bored all the time. But for now, he was happy with the way things were going, and he thought that he could easily get used to being a house husband for a while.

It made him sad at how much he'd missed about his children growing up. Having his head stuck in files all the time had meant that he'd given up too much for the job when he could have been with his family. He was going to change that as soon as today, and he wasn't going to go back to being the one who did the work so hard on cases. He'd do it if necessary, but it wasn't going to be his entire life anymore.

Tomorrow was going to be the beginning of a new life, and he was going to experience every minute of it while it lasted. His kids would just have to get used to him being around all the time, and he was sure that they'd have as much fun as he was.

~*~

It was nearly midnight when he finally went up to bed. Olivia had long since gone up to bed, and he was looking forward to snuggling up next to her. She'd be warm, and he knew that she'd be upset for a few minutes until he got as warm as she was. But he loved her and knew that she'd forgive him of just about anything. Being in love with the one person meant for you was a heady thing, he thought to himself.

He held her until she warmed him up, but he couldn't sleep. He was worried about how they were going to have money coming in with him out of work now. He nearly laughed out loud when he realized that he didn't need to work, that he had plenty of money, but old habits died hard, and he had to think of himself as a billionaire instead of the broke man that he'd been when he'd been living at home with his brothers and father.

He had to learn that his father wasn't the normal kind of man. He knew that there were other families that had the same abusive kind of life they'd had, but he never really thought about how it hadn't been the norm. It had taken him years to realize something else, too. And that was that they were lucky he'd not killed them when he could have. He certainly came close on occasion, and if not for his being put in jail a great deal, he shuddered to think what would have happened to them had he been able to roam freely like he wanted.

" You're thinking too hard." He told Olivia what he was thinking about. " In the middle of the night? I'm sure you have better things to think of than your bastard of a father. How about I tell you something good? It's not like we haven't been trying, but I'm going to have another baby. With you."

" That's the best news you could have told me. I love you." She said that she loved him as well and was happy that they could share this again. " I'll stay at home with him when you have to work."

" You're so sure it's going to be another boy, are you?" He said that they had three already and that the odds were against them in having a girl. " I think this is going to be our daughter. I'm going to keep telling myself that until she's born. You might as well get on board with it, too, as I said, she's going to be the best thing that happened to us."

" I think we've been lucky so far with the sons that we have." Olivia agreed with him and held him tightly. He put his hand on her flat belly and wished for a girl. " I wouldn't even know how to raise a daughter. With older brothers, she's going to be protected too much, I think."

" I hope so. They'll love her as much as we do." He was sure of that and decided that he couldn't love his wife any more than he did now. And he knew that he'd love her all the more tomorrow and every day after that. " I want to name her something to do with the fall season that she'll be born in. I was thinking that we name her Autumn. Autumn Martha Erickson. What do you think?"

" I love it. But just in case we should have a

boy's name in the event that we're having a son." She said that she wasn't going to jinx it and only think of having a girl. " I hope you're not too disappointed when she turns out to be a little boy again. I would love for whatever they are to be healthy and happy as you've made me all these years."

" Can you believe that we've been married almost eight years? I can't sometimes. It's like every day is a new day with you." She rolled him to his back and straddled him. " How about you make love to me, and that way we'll both sleep better. I know that I could use a good pounding."

He laughed. He couldn't help it. It made him burst out laughing when she was like this. After stripping her down to her skin, he watched as she played with her breasts. It was the most erotic thing that he'd ever seen when she was willing to show him what she needed.

Cupping her breasts with his hands, he played with her nipples as she rode him. He was hard enough to take her now, but he wanted to give her as much pleasure as she wanted. When she decided to lower herself over him, he held his cock in his hand and nearly came when she was seated over him.

" I love it when you're so hard. It makes my body hum with anticipation. I want to come a dozen times right now." She rode him slowly, and he held onto her hips. He wasn't going to rush her, but he did want to make this last. As she reached down and put her hands on his shoulders, he watched her face as she took her pleasure. When she came a second time, he rolled them over so that he was deep inside of her while he made love to her slowly. " You do this so well. I'm close to coming again. Bring me over again."

Taking her hands above her head, he held them there while his other hand ran up and down her body. Her breasts were so responsive that he wished that he could see them better in the darkened room. But he could feel her, and that was just as good. Once she was riding him again, her upward motions making him dizzy with need, he took her mouth and kissed her with all the passion that he was feeling right now. As soon as she wrapped her legs around his hips, he knew that he was going to come and come hard. Her body responded with his movements, and she cried out that she was coming. He knew that he was going to come with her when the top of his head felt like it had exploded off his shoulders, and he filled her. As he fucked her through another mind-blowing climax, she cried out again. He couldn't believe that she had come so hard after having two releases that had had her nearly passing out. He knew that he had nearly done so himself.

When he dropped atop of her, he rolled to his

side, taking her with him. Once she had settled over him, he held her tightly in his arms as she went to sleep. He couldn't sleep right away, so he did something that he'd not done in years: he played on his phone looking for something interesting to read.

At one thirty, he was ready for sleep. Olivia had long since fallen asleep into a deep sleep and he had held her throughout. Her body was so soft in all the right places that he found himself hard again. Rolling to his side so that he could watch her while he fell asleep, he thought of all the things that he was going to do now that he wasn't working.

He thought for sure that it wouldn't last long; he'd been working all his life, but he was going to enjoy it while he could. With the new baby coming along, he did worry about money, but then corrected himself. They had plenty of money to last their lifetimes together, and he had to keep telling himself that. He wondered if his brothers had the same thoughts about money and was sure that they did. They'd worked hard all their lives, and he didn't see them, him included, stopping doing that in the near future.

Waking up alone in the bed, he could hear the shower running. However, when he got up to join her in the stall, she was sitting in front of the toilet, throwing up. Getting a wet wash rag for her, he held her hair back while she vomited again. She looked up at him when she looked to be finished and smiled.

" I've never had morning sickness before. That's why I'm thinking it's a girl." He told her that her timing was a little off, but he helped her to stand. " I'm just going to take a quick shower and go back to bed. I don't feel well."

" I'll take care of the boys." Taking a shower with her, he was surprised when she was so weak. Holding her up while she washed her hair, he helped her get to bed and cover up. He was worried about her and decided that if she wasn't any better by the time he got the boys to preschool, he was going to call Locke. He might anyway. He was worried about her.

" Congratulations on the baby, and she should feel better in a couple of hours. If it lasts more than a day, bring her over, and I'll make sure she's all right. But it sounds like she has morning sickness and that's all." He thanked him. " No worries. I have been dealing with morning sickness with Alex. She's had it with all three of our daughters."

" Olivia thinks that we're having a girl and that's why she's so sick." He said that the odds were against them, but he hoped that they had a daughter. " I do too. I think after having the boys, she wants to even things out a bit."

" Alex is hoping for a son, too. I mean, instead of daughter. Not that we won't be happy with another daughter, but I think she wants one for me. To carry on my name. I don't care one way or the other, but I want her to be happy. Does that make me sound sappy?" Zander said that it did, but it was a good kind of sappy. " Whatever that means. She'll be all right. But if you're that worried, bring her over, and I'll have a look at her. It's more than likely nothing but what I said."

After getting the boys off to preschool, he was ready to face the day with nothing to do. He did have a couple of things that he hadn't finished yet, but they weren't due for a while now, and he wasn't going to rush right out and do them. Looking over the list of things that Olivia had on her list, he decided to get started on the lawn. It was a mess from the storm, and he wanted it to be nice when full summer came around. The pool was going to be used a great deal this year, and he was looking forward to having the time off to be there with his family.

Thinking about his family while he was on hold with the lawn service, he wondered what would have happened to them had they not won the lottery when they had. They'd still be in Ohio, he had no doubt, and more than likely taking menial jobs to help them get by. None of them would have gone to college to become something more, as money would have been too tight to even think about enrolling.

To him, they were just normal people who just

happened to have a great deal of money. They did things that people did, like take their kids to preschool, and worried about money. Not that they had to, but he knew that his brothers, like him, wouldn't just spend their money like they had it. Worried about when the next check was coming in was something that he did daily, and he didn't know why.

After setting up a time for the lawn crew that his brother owned to come out and assess their yard, he went to check on Olivia. She was still sleeping, but she had a bit more color in her cheeks, so he wasn't as worried as he'd been earlier. So long as she was sleeping, he knew that she'd feel better when she woke up. Otherwise, he was going to take her to his brother's home and have him run some tests.

By noon, Olivia was up and her usual self. He was glad; he'd been worried that she was sleeping so late. When she joined him in the kitchen, he went over the list of things that he'd gotten done, and she said she was proud of him. Embarrassed about that, he told her that it was his pleasure to get her list finished up, and she laughed. He joined her when she told him that she was still proud of him.

For most of the afternoon, the two of them did nothing but laze around the house. Erickson Lawn Service showed up around the time he was going to pick up the boys, and he let Olivia deal with them.

She'd know better than he did what she wanted done. He thought just cleaning up the yard would be easy, but as he was leaving, he heard her say something about getting the pool landscaping redone as well. Whatever she wanted, he was fine with that.

The boys were happy to see him picking them up. He hugged them tightly several times and wondered if they wanted to get ice cream on the way home. Excited about having something that was usually forbidden to do, he took them to the burger place around the corner from their school and got them dinner too. He knew they'd be hungry again by dinner, so he wasn't worried about them spoiling their dinner. The ice creams were a big hit for him, too.

" Daddy, will we have to go to the poor house because you quit your job?" He laughed but then realized that his son was serious. " I like my room the way it is, and some of the kids at school said I'd not be able to keep my things because the mean orphanage would take them away."

" You don't have to worry about us going to the poor house, nor you going to an orphanage." He then had to explain to them both what those two places meant. " Daddy has been saving money all his life so that we never have to worry about money again. And since both your mom and I are going to be around for a long time, you don't have to worry about us leaving you at the orphanage."

He could tell they were worried and decided to take them to the store and get them something that they'd been wanting for a long time. It was then that they were relieved that they didn't have to worry about money today, but did wonder how it had gotten around so quickly that he'd quit his job. Kids knew more than anyone thought they did. He'd heard and believed that more than ever.

Olivia was still in the kitchen with the construction boss when he decided to help the boys with their homework. He decided that practicing their letters was doing him some good, too, and had fun with the letter 'd'. He rarely wrote things down when he had his phone with him, so he was amazed at how hard it was to get letters to be perfect. They expected no less from him when he was helping them.

" How about we go out to dinner tonight?" The kids were all for that and wanted to go somewhere that had chicken nuggets. " I think we can do better than that. How about we go someplace that has a salad with our meal, and you can have two plates of it?" They were all for that. " Also, I know one place that has white milk too."

Olivia kissed him on the cheek just to make the boys gag, and it was going to be a good night for all of them. She told him that she felt better than she had, and he believed her. She looked just like she did before she'd gone to bed last night, and he was glad. He hated seeing her sick like she'd been.

After dinner, the boys were exhausted and were easy to put to bed. He read them a couple of lines of their books, and they were asleep. Going to the living room to be with Olivia, he wondered what the next twenty years would bring and decided that he was going to take it one day at a time. It was the only way to live, he told himself, and he was happy to have his family right here with him.

Before You Go...

HELP AN AUTHOR

write a review

THANK YOU!

Share your voice and help guide other readers to these wonderful books. Even if it's only a line or two, your reviews help readers discover the author's books so they can continue creating stories that you'll love. Log in to your favorite retailer and leave a review. Thank you.

Kathi S. Barton is an award-winning and bestselling author known for her steamy paranormal romances and unforgettable characters. A recipient of the prestigious Pinnacle Book Achievement Award, her books have topped the charts on Amazon and All Romance eBooks, earning her a loyal global readership.

Kathi lives in Nashport, Ohio, with her husband, Paul. When she's not crafting passionate love stories set in magical worlds, she enjoys camping, exploring local auctions, and attending county fairs, where Paul showcases his artwork and pottery. Her creative spark—fueled by a muse she describes as a cross between Jimmy Stewart and Hugh Jackman—brings her stories to vivid, heartfelt life.

Paranormal romance with plenty of heat is her favorite genre, and she loves connecting with her readers. Feel free to reach out—Kathi would love to hear from you.

Email: aaronskiss@gmail.com

Follow Kathi on her blog: http://kathisbartonauthor.blogspot.com/

www.ingramcontent.com/pod-product-compliance
Lightning Source LLC
LaVergne TN
LVHW090515110826
845146LV00003B/860

* 9 7 9 8 8 9 1 2 6 5 1 2 7 *